the scarlet letterman

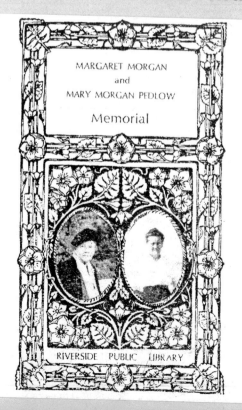

Also by Cara Lockwood
Wuthering High

the scarlet letterman

a bard academy novel

cara lockwood

POCKET BOOKS   MTV BOOKS

New York   London   Toronto   Sydney

POCKET BOOKS, a division of Simon & Schuster, Inc.
1230 Avenue of the Americas, New York, NY 10020

ISBN-13: 978-1-4165-2490-8
ISBN-10:   1-4165-2490-8

This MTV Books/Pocket Books trade paperback edition January 2007

10 9 8 7 6 5 4 3 2 1

For information regarding special discounts for bulk purchases, please contact Simon & Schuster Special Sales at 1-800-456-6798 or business@simonandschuster.com

For all my English teachers

Acknowledgments

Many thanks to my ingenious friend, Elizabeth Kinsella, who named this book. She's got the market cornered on clever. Thanks to my family: Mom, Dad, Matt, and my husband, Daren. A special thanks to my editor, Lauren McKenna, and my agent, Deidre Knight, and everyone at the Knight Agency. Much appreciation goes to my Bard Academy promotional varsity team: Kate Miller, Kate Kinsella, Shannon Whitehead, Christina Swartz, Jane Ricordati, Carroll Jordan, Stacey Causey, Linda Newman, Stacey Cohen, Kelly Ballarini, and Mary Chalfant.

the scarlet letterman

One

I should be happy.

I am wearing Ryan Kent's letterman jacket, which means that it's official, we're dating (in fact, as of today, it's been six weeks, two days, and four hours—not that I'm counting or anything). Ryan Kent, for those of you who might be blind, is a state championship basketball player who happens to be Bard Academy's reigning Sexiest Boy Alive, and is, as of this moment, my boyfriend.

That's me, sitting in the stands of the Bard Academy gym, wearing the Bard Academy uniform along with some of my signature touches (leggings and lots of accessories). I watch as Ryan Kent sails above his competitors and dunks the basketball *again*. After he smashes the basketball into the basket, he gives me a wink and a wave as he travels back down to the other end of the court.

Coach H shouts at Ryan to stop "showboating," but that's like telling Ryan Kent not to be gorgeous. It's just not in his genetic makeup.

I feel like I should be in a teen movie. You know, one of those movies where the not-so-popular, nerdy girl gets a makeover and finds herself with the star of the basketball team. Granted, I've never been nerdy, but I'm not exactly prom queen material, either. I'm the artsy, thrift-store girl. Typically not the one who lands the most popular boy in school.

So, like I said, I should be happy. And I am happy. Well, *mostly* happy, except for the fact that I'm not. Entirely.

And I don't know why exactly.

Yes, it's true I'm back at Bard Academy, delinquent boarding school, but it's not that. I know I'm going to risk sounding like "that poor girl with the amazingly cute boyfriend" when I say this, but something is just not right.

And yes, that "something" has a name.

It's Heathcliff.

And I can't believe I'm dating one boy and thinking about another. I never in a million years pegged myself as one of those boy-crazy girls. The ones who desperately believe in a soul mate, except that said soul mate changes every day. Granted, I change accessories every day, but I thought I'd be less fickle when it came to romance.

Apparently, I'm not.

Because the more I try to just think about Ryan, the more I end up thinking about Heathcliff, which I know is wrong, wrong, *wrong*.

Liz, my friend from my old school, would say I'm sabotaging myself. That secretly, I think I don't deserve Ryan Kent, and that I *do* deserve bad-boy-to-the-core Heathcliff, so I'm trying to make that happen by tanking my relationship with Ryan. She calls this phenomenon Trading Down. It's why, she thinks, she's got serious sex-impulse control problems (meaning that she'll just as easily have sex with a boy as she would let one open the door for her because no matter who she's with she feels she doesn't deserve them).

But maybe I *am* trying to trade down, and I don't even know it.

It's true that I never actually pictured myself with the captain of the basketball team type, the Should-Be-a-Recurring-Character-on-*The OC* guy. I always thought guys like Ryan had girlfriends like . . . well, like Parker Rodham, who is currently glaring daggers at me from the basketball court sidelines. She and her clones are in cheerleading outfits, and Parker keeps doing the splits in an obvious attempt to get Ryan's attention.

It isn't working and that's making her mad.

I could deal with her. What I can't deal with is the fact that Heathcliff is MIA. I haven't seen him since last semester. This from the boy who told me I was his whole life. The only evidence I have that he exists at all is the necklace he sent me, the one that I wear around my neck.

The necklace reminds me that there's another problem with Heathcliff: He's not even real. He's a fictional character from *Wuthering Heights* who happens to be stuck in *this* world. That's right. I'm obsessing about a *fictional* character from 1847. Where do I start with what's wrong with that? Not to mention the minor detail that him being here at all makes our dimension unstable. Confused? Welcome to my world.

"Is that a new necklace or something?" Hana asks me as she leans over, catching me fumbling with Heathcliff's locket. Inside there's a single piece of a page of the original copy of *Wuthering Heights*, which is the only thing keeping him in this world, as far as I know. Should it be destroyed, he'd be sent back to 1847.

Hana straightens the black-framed glasses she wears and puts down the book she brought to read at the game. Hana is never without reading material. She's what I would call a Lit Nerd, although in a good way. She's like walking CliffsNotes.

"No," I say, dumping the necklace quickly into my shirt again, hiding it away. I feel a twinge of guilt for thinking about Heathcliff when I'm wearing Ryan's jacket. And besides, Hana doesn't even know that Heathcliff is still alive.

I can't tell her or anyone else about him. For one, she's not his biggest fan (since he kidnapped her, Samir, and Blade last semester). But secondly, he was supposed to have disappeared for good, but he didn't. And I am in possession of the only thing that can send him back—the tiny remnant of the original *Wuthering Heights*. If the teachers found out, they'd demand he be put back into the pages of *Wuthering Heights*. It's probably why he's keeping a low profile. He doesn't want to be zapped back to 1847.

And yes, you don't have to tell me how insane it is that I'm fantasizing about a fictional character when I have a real-life boyfriend right in front of me, who has just sat down on the bench and has taken off his sweaty jersey and is changing into a new, nonsweaty one. One who isn't, technically, 160 years old.

"By the way, did I tell you that I'm not jealous that you and Ryan are dating?" Hana asks me.

"Only about a zillion times. I think it's pretty clear you *are* jealous," I say.

"Yes, but if I say it enough times, maybe it'll be true," Hana says.

"Oh, please," Samir scoffs. "What does Ryan Kent have that I haven't got?"

Ryan pulls his new jersey over his championship triceps and whips his glistening blond hair out of his eyes. He's just played nearly an entire game of basketball and he's still shoot-ready for a Hollister ad.

"You have to be kidding me, right?" Hana asks Samir, giving him a playful shove.

"I can't believe you're wearing Ryan's jacket," Samir says. "That's so, like, 1985. I mean, who does that anymore?"

"You're just jealous you don't have a letterman jacket to *give*," Hana says to Samir.

"Not to mention someone actually willing to wear it," I add.

"Look, we all know that you're just dating Ryan to make me jealous," Samir says. "And, okay, it's working, so let's give up this charade." Samir grabs my hand and pretends to land slobbery kisses on it. Samir is always trying to see how far he can get.

"Gross," I say, pulling my hand away.

"Don't listen to him," Hana says.

"And when do I listen to him?" I ask her.

"Would you guys be quiet? Some of us are *trying* to watch the game," huffs Blade, my quirky, occult-obsessed roommate, who despite her oddities isn't actually all that bad. For the spring semester, and in honor of Valentine's Day next week, she's dyed her hair pink. She's also put a sparkly barrette in it. Granted, it's a skull and crossbones, but still. It's a start.

"Since when are you into sports?" Samir asks Blade.

"Since Number Thirty-one started playing," Hana adds. Number Thirty-one is a geeky, lanky boy who plays center on Ryan's team, and Blade's current love infatuation.

Samir's face falls a little. I know he was hoping that Blade's short-lived crush on him would last longer than a month, but Blade has moved on. And given Number Thirty-one's awkward appearance (and Samir's definite built-in geek factor), my Goth roomie has a thing for nerds.

More than half of the Bard Academy student body is sitting in the bleachers watching the basketball game. There isn't much to do at a boarding school for delinquents stuck on a remote island off the coast of Maine where pagers, cellphones, televisions, and iPods are forbidden. As a result, school sporting events are always well attended.

The opposing team is some boys' prep school in Maine. Even our rival teams have to be ferried to our island (appropriately named Shipwreck Island, since one hundred years ago it was a magnet for ships in storms, but it's also apropos today because most of us feel like castaways). I heard some of the rival players calling our island "Alcatraz," because of all the stories about the delinquent students here. Apparently they're only one of about three boarding schools still willing to play us. Parents don't like their Harvard wannabes mixing with the wrong crowd.

"You know, it's good to see you with Ryan, though, seriously," Hana says. "I thought for a while you might be holding a torch for Heathcliff."

"Heathcliff?" I say loudly. Too loudly. I dial down a notch. "Why would I be holding a torch for Heathcliff? I mean, how is he my type?"

I'm secretly hoping this leads to a long discussion about Heathcliff. Maybe hearing Hana tick off his bad points will help me shake my obsession with him. Of course, if I'm honest with myself, I just really want the excuse to talk about him. And that can't be good.

Hana studies me for a beat or two. Has she caught on? Does she know I'm secretly wearing his necklace and pining for the boy who nearly got her killed?

"No reason," she says, and then falls silent.

I can't help but feel disappointed. I wanted to talk more about him, and now the moment is lost.

"Uh-oh, looks like Ms. W is leaking again," Samir says, nodding over in the direction of the Bard faculty section where Ms. W and Headmaster B are watching the game. It's true. Ms. W has a wet sleeve again. It's dripping onto the bleacher in front of her.

I wave at Ms. W, get her attention, and then point to my own sleeve. Startled, Ms. W looks down and then the water mark disappears.

"Is it just me, or are our teachers getting careless?" Samir asks. "I saw Coach H glide through a wall in the boys' dorm last night. He's lucky that nobody but me saw him. And to think they're so clumsy after they gave us that big lecture."

Samir is talking about the end of last semester when Headmaster B sat the four of us all down and swore us all to eternal silence about the Big Secret, which is the fact that all of our teachers are dead. They're ghosts—and not just any ghosts, they're famous literary figures stuck in purgatory for either taking their own lives or dying before their time. Headmaster B made us all swear not to tell any other student on campus about the Big Secret. I mean, like we *would*. You know, because we're so likely to be believed. The swearing part is really unnecessary. Try telling someone at boarding school that you know that their teacher is really Virginia Woolf or Charlotte Brontë. It's not the sort of thing that's going to win you friends.

"I think something is up with them," Hana says. "They seem distracted, don't you think? Like something is bothering them."

"You mean aside from the fact that they're dead

and stuck in purgatory with a bunch of adolescents?" Samir asks.

"We ought to form some kind of society—the four of us," Blade says. "You know, a secret society to help protect them from themselves."

"A secret society?" Hana asks, skeptical.

"We could call ourselves the LITs—Literary Investigation Team."

"That is the dumbest thing I've ever heard," Hana says.

"I think it's kind of cool," Samir says. "You're just jealous you didn't think of that acronym first, Ms. Bookworm."

"Whatever," Hana says, dismissive, as she adjusts her black-framed glasses. "You can't seriously think we ought to form our own secret club," Hana adds. "I mean, are we twelve? Miranda, what do you think?"

But I'm not paying attention. I'm busy watching the tall guy in the hooded sweatshirt, the one that has his face nearly entirely covered, the one who snuck in through the side door of the gym and is now milling about, arms crossed, on the left side of the bleachers across from us. Something about his shape looks familiar. Tall, broad, and brooding. Could it be Heathcliff?

"Miranda? Hello?" Hana says, snapping her fingers.

"Forget her," Samir says. "She's too busy looking at her Man Meat." This is what Samir calls Ryan Kent.

"Besides, I don't know if Miranda would be eligible for membership in LITs," Blade says. "You know, because she is one-sixteenth fiction."

Blade is referring to the fact that my great-great-great-great-grandmother was Catherine from *Wuthering Heights*. It's a very weird piece of information that I'm only just starting to digest. Apparently one of Catherine's children managed to cross over to our world and did the deed with my great-great-great-grandfather, and now, here I am. The descendant of somebody who began as a figment of a writer's imagination. Don't ask me how it all works, I'm still trying to figure it out myself. All I know is that my middle name—Earnshaw—means I'm related to one of the most famous characters in literature. I keep waiting to see what else I find out while I'm at Bard. Was Hamlet my uncle? Anything is possible here.

"That's racist," Hana says.

"You mean fictionist," Samir corrects.

"Anyway, Miranda would have to be in the club or I wouldn't join," Hana adds.

"Would there be meetings? Because I definitely don't do meetings," Samir says.

I watch the hooded figure at the back of the gym make his way closer to the faculty section. If that *is* Heathcliff, he's playing a dangerous game. He has few friends among the faculty. As far as I know, if any of them knew he was still walking among us, they'd want to see him banished—for good. I'm not even watching Ryan now as he scores a three-point shot at the buzzer. Everyone in the bleachers stands to cheer, and I temporarily lose sight of the Hooded Sweatshirt Guy.

"I'll be right back," I tell Hana, trying to push my way through the crowd and down to the floor. Hooded Sweatshirt Guy is making his way out of the gym. I feel an urgent need to catch him. Is it Heathcliff? Could it be? I can't tell. I need a closer look.

I'm caught up in a mini crowd cluster, and have to push through to get to the gym doors. I swing them open, and suddenly I'm standing outside in the cold February air. Alone.

TWO

If Heathcliff came this way, he didn't leave any tracks. There's a fresh blanket of white snow on the ground with no footprints. On the snow in front of me there's a scrap of paper. I kneel down to pick it up.

It's just white art paper with part of a drawing on it. It looks like half of a triangle of sorts. I can't really tell what it is. It's too small.

"Miranda? There you are," says Ryan Kent, surprising me. Without thinking, I put the piece of paper in my pocket. "I thought I saw you come this way. Why didn't you stop to say hello?"

"Oh, uh, I mean, I was going to, but I needed some fresh air," I say. "Um, you know, too much boy sweat in there."

"Since when do you not like boy sweat?" Ryan says,

grabbing me and shaking his sweaty head so that I'm showered with sweat drops.

"Ew!" I squeal, but he's got his arms around me, and then he pushes me up against the side of the gym and lands a kiss on my lips.

And for a second I forget about Heathcliff, Bard, and everything else, and I'm sucked into that kissing-a-cute-boy vortex where time stands still and everything around me freezes. Ryan Kent is a fantastic kisser.

When he pulls away, I'm a little breathless.

I glance up at Ryan, and then over his shoulder, to the woods, where there's a flash of movement. I think it's Hooded Sweatshirt Guy, but I can't be sure. Did he see me kissing Ryan? There's no way to tell. I can't see anyone near the trees now.

"Come on," Ryan says, taking me by the hand and leading me off to the trees.

"But the rules," I say, thinking about how we're not supposed to go into the forest at night. And Heathcliff might be there. And while I'm dying to see him, I have no idea how he'd react to Ryan, who's at this moment, squeezing my hand.

"This is our only time together. We've got twenty minutes till curfew," he says, picking up the pace and taking me along. "We probably won't even be missed for fifteen."

Having a boyfriend at a delinquent boarding school is difficult, it's true. It's not like we can go on dates, or be alone for extended periods. There are Guardians everywhere, and faculty, too, and so even kissing can be a challenge.

"But . . ." I don't tell him what I'm really thinking. The woods are really seriously creepy. I know now that Bard is purgatory, and that most of the ghosts here don't really mean us harm, but that doesn't mean that I'm willing to hang out in the dark woods at night with a full moon over our heads and not get a little wigged out.

Still, Ryan is determined. He's got that look on his face that all boys get when they want to get some. And, honestly, I'm not sure what makes me more nervous. The idea of being stuck in the woods, or whatever Ryan is hoping I'm going to do. Like I said before, my friend Liz is the one with the experience. I have no idea what I'm doing.

It's so cold, my hands feel numb, but Ryan squeezes my hand and glances back at me as he leads me deeper into the woods. I wonder what's going to happen. Are we just going to make out? Will I have to do something else? I'm so totally clueless in this department, it's seriously sad.

Which is why Liz says I ought to live with the Amish. She acts like I'm the only girl in America who hasn't given it up yet, but I know there are others out there. I can't be the only one.

I tell myself to calm down. Aren't I crazy about Ryan? And wouldn't almost any girl in class love to trade places with me?

Ryan stops now, and turns. He's got a snowball in his hand. He whirls it at me, and it hits me straight on the forehead.

"Oh, you're *dead*," I say, grabbing a bunch of snow from the ground and putting together a hapless snowball. I head after him, managing to hit him dead in the face. He laughs, and spits out new snow, even as he grabs a handful of snow on the ground and lunges at me, grabbing me by the waist and pinning me against a tree. As I squirm to get free, he shoves snow down the back of my Bard jacket and shirt collar. The snow is freezing as it drips down my back.

"Aaaaaaaaaack, you *jerk*!" I squeal at him, but I'm laughing, too. I can't help it. Ryan is just *fun*. The anxiety I felt before is completely gone, and now I'm just with Ryan and it feels good.

Ryan gets a semiserious look on his face and leans in for a kiss. But instead of feeling swept up in the moment, I feel a hard piece of bark jabbing my back.

"Wait, ow," I say, pushing against him a little, and he eases his weight off me a little, backing up.

"What's wrong?" he asks, suddenly worried.

cara lockwood

"It's just the tree . . . and . . . it's cold . . ." God, I'm blowing it. I sound as whiny as my kid sister Lindsay.

"Not the best make-out spot is it?" Ryan asks me. I'm glad he agrees.

"Bard is very short on those," I say.

"I guess I'll have to write an official complaint." Ryan leans in to kiss me again, but before his lips touch mine, I hear a sudden crack. Like a footstep on a twig.

"What was that?" I ask him, turning my head toward the noise.

"What was what?" he asks me, dipping and nuzzling my neck. I hear another cracking sound. It sounds like something very large and very heavy is walking in the forest. I think suddenly of Hooded Sweatshirt Guy. What if that wasn't Heathcliff at all, but some psycho killer with an ax? There's another crunching sound. Whatever is out there is getting closer.

This time Ryan hears it, too. His head snaps up. I try to focus on the trees, but I can't make out anything but dark blobs.

The whole scene just smacks of a horror movie. Didn't Jason kill people who were making out?

"It's probably just a bear," Ryan says.

"I hope you are kidding," I say.

"I am. Bears are hibernating now, aren't they?"

Ryan takes his attention away from the forest and turns back to me. "Come on, we only have a few minutes before Coach H comes looking for me."

Ryan starts to lean in, but I put my hand on his chest.

"I think we'd better go," I say. I'm not at all sure it's safe to be here anymore.

"Come on, one more minute," Ryan says.

"Ryan, I'm serious. I think something is out there. I think we need to go."

"Where?" he asks, looking out over my head to the forest behind us.

And that's when, over Ryan's shoulder, I see two eyes peering out from the darkness. They're glowing red.

"Behind you!" I stutter.

But when Ryan turns, the eyes disappear.

"I-I-I saw something," I say, already moving away from Ryan. "Let's get out of here."

"Miranda, come on."

"I'm *serious*," I say. "I don't care if you want to stay, but I'm going."

And then, almost as if someone else were reading my mind, I hear a high-pitched scream.

Three

Ryan and I both start, and then, without saying a word, we both run toward the sound of the scream.

When we clamber out of the forest, we see Parker, down on the ground, surrounded by two of her clone posse. Parker is looking a little disheveled and clearly out of it.

"What happened?" Ryan asks, a wrinkle of worry forming in his forehead. I don't like that wrinkle. And I certainly don't like that Parker is causing it.

"She was *nearly raped*," says one of the clones.

"By who?" I ask.

"Some guy, I didn't see his face," Parker sputters. "He cornered me, just here, and he slammed me against the wall . . ."

Something about this situation doesn't feel right to me, and not only the fact that Parker is a known pathological liar. I can't help but think it's quite the co-incidence that Ryan disappears with me for a make-out session, and Parker conveniently gets attacked. Okay, this is evil of me, I know, but it's *Parker* we're talking about. No tactic is beneath her. She's been coveting Ryan since he came to Bard, and she'd be willing to do anything to get his attention.

"We should call a Guardian," I say. "Report him."

"No," Parker says, giving me a sharp look. "I'm okay."

Bingo, I think. She doesn't want to report it to the authorities because maybe it didn't happen?

"What did he look like?" Ryan asks, kneeling down so he's nearly at eye level with Parker.

"She *said* she didn't see his face," the other clone says.

"I don't know," Parker adds. "He was wearing a hooded sweatshirt and it was dark."

"Hooded sweatshirt?" I echo, my attention sud-denly focused on Parker's every word. "You're sure he wore a hooded sweatshirt? Was it blue?"

"Um, yeah, why? Was he one of your friends?" Parker snaps.

Ryan and Parker's clones are now looking at me.

"Not exactly," I say. "I just saw a guy in the gym, wearing a sweatshirt. But lots of guys do." Could Heathcliff have shoved Parker? He doesn't like her, that's for certain, but I didn't think he would ever try to rape her or anyone else. Would he?

"Ryan, would you mind walking us back to the dorm? I don't feel safe out here," Parker says, rubbing her own arms and shivering.

Ryan doesn't even glance at me. "Of course," he says, helping Parker to her feet. When she stumbles a little, he puts an arm around her. So that only I can see, Parker sends me a smug smile.

By the end of the week, word about Parker's attacker circulates like wildfire through the campus. It doesn't help that on Wednesday one of Parker's clones also claims to have been attacked by the Hooded Sweatshirt Stalker. By Friday, there's an all-out security alert on campus for the would-be rapist, and there are posters even, with a drawing of Parker's attacker, who looks a lot like the Unibomber. So much for Parker insisting on keeping this quiet. I guess she decided to tell the teachers after all.

"Do you believe the lengths Parker will go to for a little attention?" Hana asks me as we watch her clones hand out fliers on campus.

"So you don't think she was attacked, either?" I ask Hana, surprised.

"Do *you*?" Hana asks me.

"I don't know." Hana and I watch as Parker is

trailed by Ryan, who is helping her carry a box of flyers to the library.

"She gets attacked while you are sucking face with your boyfriend and then said boyfriend suddenly becomes her twenty-four/seven errand boy and you don't find that suspicious?"

"She's scared to walk around campus without an escort," I say.

"So why does the escort have to be *your* boyfriend?" Hana says.

"I know." I sigh. "I don't know what I can do about it, though. Anytime I bring it up with Ryan, he acts like I'm being insensitive."

"Maybe you should remind him that Parker poisoned her own mother. I think her stalker has more to fear from her than vice versa."

Before I can reply, the Bard school bus churns and lurches into view at the other end of the snowy campus commons.

"Watch out," Hana says. "It's the driver's ed class."

As we look on, the bus careens into some nearby bushes, nearly hitting two students, before coming to a skidding stop about ten feet from us.

Behind the wheel is a white-faced Samir, who looks like he just went on a roller coaster without being buckled in. Thompson, our driver's ed teacher, stumbles out of the bus and declares, "Now *that's* what I call crazy mad parallel parking!"

"You do know that you're in the middle of the commons?" I ask Thompson.

He frowns at me. "Details, details," he murmurs.

"How can he possibly be qualified to teach driver's ed?" I whisper to Hana.

"I don't know, but I'm taking it in special session next week," she says. "Aren't you? Isn't your birthday in March?"

"My dad would never sign off on me taking it," I say. "And they require both parents to give permission."

"But you won't be able to take your driver's test when you get back home this summer without some driver's ed."

"I know," I say. "I've written to my dad a hundred times. I think he doesn't even read my letters. But even if he did, I seriously doubt he'd give me permission. First of all, I totaled his car. And second, the man doesn't *like* me."

"That's just because you're the only one who calls him on his BS," Hana says.

"Exactly. And there's so much of it. I mean, the way he goes through wives, he should just rent his next spouse from Blockbuster. It'll save him all those settlement fees," I say. Dad left my mom, sister, and me for his secretary five years ago. He's divorced and remarried since then. As far as I'm concerned, he's doing his best to pretend that I, his firstborn, don't exist.

"Yo! Heathcliff!" I hear someone behind us call. Without thinking, I whip around.

I find myself searching frantically for the tall, broad, and brooding figure of Heathcliff, but instead I just see two skater types trying to do jumping tricks on the stairwell near the library sans skateboards, using only the soles of their tennis shoes.

"Looking for someone?" Hana asks, eyeing me with some suspicion.

I shake my head just as the bell tower tolls, signaling the end of lunch. "I've got to go see Ms. W," I say, leaving Hana standing near the bus.

On my way to my counseling session, I walk close to the library, near where the skater types are flinging themselves off the railings.

"Hey," I ask the one who sails into the air and lands on bended knee in front of the stairs. His hair is dyed red, with long bangs in front and a cropped, shaved cut in back. "Do you know Heathcliff?"

"Do we know him? Dude—*everyone* knows him," the skater says.

Heathcliff's reputation at Bard was made last semester when he single-handedly took down three Bard Guardians, the glorified mall security guards that keep us delinquents in line. Heathcliff knocked out three of them in the cafeteria and escaped in front of nearly the entire school. In his absence, his legend has only grown, and he's about to join the league of Campus Legends, which include Kate Shaw's Ghost and the Haunted Library.

"But have you seen him? I mean, lately?"

He looks at me as if I've taken one too many bong hits.

"But you called his name?"

"Dude, that's a mad move, 'the Heathcliff,' " he says. "I'll show you." He rears up, jumps on the staircase railing, and slides down it like he's skating, and then does a flip at the end, landing on his feet at the bottom of the stairs.

"That, dude, is a 'Yo! Heathcliff.' "

"So you haven't seen him?" I can't help but be disappointed.

"No," he says, shaking his head. "You heard the rumor, right? Headmaster sent him to juvie."

That's one rumor that I know isn't true. You can't send a fictional character to juvenile detention. But where is he? And why is he staying away from me? Maybe if I knew what had happened to him, then I wouldn't be so obsessed with him.

Four

"Thinking about Heathcliff?" Ms. W asks me, zeroing in on my thoughts with uncanny precision like she always does. I'm sitting in her office where I've appeared for my monthly counseling session, during which we normally talk about how I feel about my complicated relationship with my absentee dad. But lately we've been talking more and more about Heathcliff and about my fictional ancestor and about coping with that.

"Is it that obvious?" I ask her.

"It was the book that clued me in," Ms. W says, nodding toward my backpack, where my dog-eared copy of *Wuthering Heights* is sticking out. "You're never without it. How many times have you read it now?"

I shrug. "A couple," I say, although it was probably

closer to a dozen. The book is my only insight into Heathcliff. I can't decide if he's a good person or a bad person, but the book is all I have to explain him.

"You know, it's okay that you miss him," Ms. W says.

"It is?" I ask, surprised. "I thought you hated him."

"I don't hate him. I don't think he's good for you, but I don't hate him. I think he belongs in his world and not ours. I do see that the two of you had a strong connection."

"You think we have a strong connection?"

"Had, Miranda. Not *have*," Ms. W corrects. "It's natural for you to feel strongly about someone who saved your life. He put himself in danger to rescue you more than once, and you're likely to feel a sense of obligation. But don't confuse that sense of obligation with something deeper than that."

"But why—" I start, and then stop myself. I was going to ask her why, if he was willing to risk his life to save me, now he didn't seem to want to talk to me. I can't believe I almost blurted out the secret that Heathcliff was still alive in this world.

"Why what?"

Quickly, I try to cover up my near mistake. "Why does he have to stay in *Wuthering Heights*?"

"You know he can't live in this world permanently," Ms. W says. "If he did, he'd disappear from *Wuthering*

Heights, and think about all the people who would miss knowing him. In fact, the entire book might disappear forever without him in it."

"I know," I say, having heard this before. "And having him here makes our dimensions unstable, I know, but if my great-great-great-grandmother managed to live in our world her whole life . . ."

"Elizabeth Linton, the fictional daughter of Catherine and your ancestor, was a minor character in the book, and her absence is not missed in the story," Ms. W tells me curtly. "By the time you read the book, she was completely gone from it, and that was fine. Her twin sister Catherine lived on in the book and moves the story forward. But without Heathcliff, there *is* no *Wuthering Heights.* We don't know what would happen if a major character managed to make the leap from fiction to reality. It could be catastrophic."

". . . and bring on the Apocalypse?" Everything around here seems to cause the end of the world.

"Maybe," Ms. W says, evasive. "We don't know for sure."

I sigh, frustrated.

"Miranda, there's something else we need to talk about," Ms. W says, her eyes darting back and forth as if she's about to tell me something she shouldn't. She nods at the door and it closes with a click. I'm still not sure about all her ghost powers, but it appears they include walking through walls and moving objects with her mind. It's not something I think I'll ever quite get used to.

"The faculty are concerned about you," she says, her voice at a low-pitched whisper. "You and your friends. They don't like the idea of students knowing about . . . us and about . . . the vault."

The vault is the special room beneath the library where all of Bard's Books with Powers are kept. If taken from the vault, characters from them can come to life. Like Heathcliff, my great-great-great-grandma, or not so nice ones, like Dracula or Frankenstein. They also hold the souls of the faculty ghosts, and if you destroy the books, you destroy the teachers.

I can see why they might be nervous about students knowing this particular secret. It would be like if you found out your principal was Superman, and you knew the location of two tons of kryptonite.

"I can understand that, but really, your secret is safe with us," I say.

"I know that, because I know you and your friends," Ms. W says. "But the others aren't so sure."

"Who?" I ask, wondering if it's Headmaster B. She definitely wasn't keen on us finding out the truth.

"I can't tell you, but you and your friends need to be careful," Ms. W says. "For one, stay away from the vault."

"We weren't planning on going near it," I say. "None of us wants to see a reappearance of Dracula."

"Good," Ms. W says, looking a little relieved. "Just keep a low profile this semester and do well in school, and I'm sure the other faculty will come around."

I'm not sure who she's trying to convince more—her or me.

Five

"That totally sucks," says Blade that night during our study time. Every evening from 8:00 P.M. (curfew) to 10:00 P.M. (lights out), we're confined to our rooms, where our choices are study or sleep. "They don't *trust* us? But we saved their ghostly butts last semester."

"Tell me about it," I say.

"This just proves they're not just dead, they're crazy," Blade says. "I mean, take Mr. B, my American history teacher. He talks to invisible people."

Mr. B is William Blake, the poet. I'd heard rumors about him before. Most of the students think he's on drugs, because he talks to himself, and on occasion, people who aren't actually there.

I want to ask her more about Blake—even talking to Blade is preferable to reading one more chapter on the

Puritans. But, before I can, I hear the footsteps of the Rat Patrol in the hall, and so both of us swivel to the front and pretend to be studying. The Rat Patrol is a group of Guardians who patrol the dorms and the campus grounds to make sure that no student is out of their room during mandatory study time.

I hate study time. It's two hours of sitting in complete silence. I can barely find the stamina to watch two hours of *Laguna Beach*, much less do something like read. But at this point, I would literally kill someone just to hear ten minutes of a radio. Even if it was a country station. That's how desperate I am for a sound other than the wind blowing against our window.

It's enough to make me want to cry, I'm so bored. For the first ten minutes of study time, I read and reread the letters from home—one from my friend Liz, and one from Mom. I reread them each ten times. That's how desperate I am for entertainment. Liz, bless her, has taken it upon herself to give me TV updates, so I can almost imagine the finale of *Veronica Mars*. As usual, though, there's no letter from Dad. He's still pissed that I wrecked his new BMW, but I don't really care. I was trying to save Lindsay from a school bully, which is technically his job anyway. Besides, Dad took the insurance money and bought a Range Rover, so it's not like he's got a right to have a pity party. Not when I'm stuck on Shipwreck Island without even so much as a single copy of *Teen People*.

Thinking about Dad makes my blood pressure rise, so I put him out of my head and focus on Liz's loopy handwriting, which calms me. She's giving her own opinion about her new must-see show, *My Super Sweet 16* on MTV. The last part of her letter outlines what she would do with $100,000 instead of throwing a lame birthday party. This reminds me that my own birthday is coming up in little over a month. I'm going to spend my sweet sixteen in purgatory with a bunch of ghost teachers. This thought makes me hate my dad even more.

"God, I'm *bored*." Blade sighs, voicing my own thoughts. She throws up her hands and shuts the book on her desk. "I'm going to bed," she declares.

"It's only eight-thirty," I point out. At this rate, she'll get eleven hours of sleep.

"I'm either going to sleep, or slip into an ennui coma," Blade says. "And I prefer sleep. My dreams, at least, can be like television."

Blade falls right to sleep, but I can't sleep until lights out at 10:00. And even then, I lie awake thinking about Heathcliff. Did he attack Parker? Is he even still alive? Maybe the piece of paper in my locket isn't enough to keep him in this world. Maybe he's faded to oblivion like his creator, Emily Brontë, who disappeared after most of her book was destroyed last semester.

With all these questions swirling around in my head, I fall into a fitful sleep, and I dream about Heathcliff.

He's carrying me in his arms, just like he did when he saved me from a fire in the library last semester. His arms are strong and thick, and I feel like I can stay there forever. His eyes are the same—dark and ambiguous—and as usual, I don't know what he's thinking.

He's taking me deep into the woods, just like Ryan did, but this time Heathcliff doesn't stop until he takes me to a river. He puts me down by a horseshoe-shaped tree, and disappears into the forest. Alone suddenly, I know something very bad is coming, and when I look up, I see the two red eyes again, peering at me.

Distantly I hear Heathcliff call for help, but I can't get to him somehow, and I know he won't be able to help me. I have to face whatever is attached to those eyes alone.

The eyes start to move closer to me, and that's when I wake up, cold sweat trickling down my back. I find myself nearly face-to-face with a white demon, and that's when I realize I'm facing the window and looking at the gargoyle sitting on the ledge.

My heart nearly leaps out of my throat before I realize I'm just at Bard, where the campus decor is like Fright Fest.

The full moonlight glints off the gargoyle's sharp fangs. I shiver and turn away. One of these days I'll remember to go to sleep with the blinds down. No wonder I'm having nightmares. In the dark, Blade snorts and rolls over, then begins a loud chain of snores. It's one of the few times I've been glad that Blade snores. There's something reassuring about a roommate who can sleep through nearly anything.

I think back to the short-lived two-week Christmas break, back when I slept in a room decorated with pink gingham, and I wonder if I'm ever going to get back to a place where I can peacefully sleep through the night without dreaming about monsters. There's one thing about Bard that never changes. It always seems to give me nightmares.

I'm awake now, and I know I won't be able to go back to sleep. I creep over to my desk, careful not to make any sudden sounds, even though I doubt anything would wake Blade up. I pull my backpack off my chair.

Blade snorts in her sleep, and I temporarily freeze. When she shifts under the covers and starts snoring again, I grab my dog-eared copy of *Wuthering Heights,* the one I've read and reread, and flip to the middle of the book, where I keep the note Heathcliff sent me.

Delicately I unfold it, taking in Heathcliff's shaky handwriting, and rereading it for the thousandth time.

"You are my soul. So long as you exist, so do I. Yours forever, H."

I trace the H with my finger. I can't believe he'd just stop talking to me. Not after sending me this note. I think about his thick dark hair and mysterious eyes.

Where *is* he?

Six

"Did you hear? There was another attack of the Hooded Sweatshirt Stalker," says Blade the next morning over breakfast (something lumpy, yellow, and watery that may or may not have been an egg-based product).

"You can't be *serious*," Hana sniffs. She still does not believe the Hooded Sweatshirt Stalker exists. She thinks Parker is making it all up.

"Who did he attack?" I ask, all the while wondering if that *is* Heathcliff what in the world is he doing?

"Some girl, who apparently didn't know Parker," Blade says. "I overheard the story in the shower this morning. This girl—her name was Amanda or something—was with the crew team, and was walking down by the river where they practice. She said this guy jumped out of nowhere and knocked her down."

"We've got a crew team?" I ask.

"Duh," Blade says. "Anyway, that's it. He was wearing a hooded sweatshirt, but she didn't see his face. Just like Parker."

"So there wasn't a rape?"

"No rape. Nothing like that. Just shoving."

"So why is everyone calling him a stalker? He should be called a shover," Hana says.

"You still don't believe Parker is telling the truth?" Blade asks.

"I just think it's all a bit convenient," Hana says. "Right, Miranda?"

"Um, yeah, right," I say, wondering if my suspicions about the Hooded Sweatshirt Stalker are right. Is he Heathcliff? And if so, should I tell someone? But who?

I decide I can't be sure if it's Heathcliff. After all, I didn't see his face, either.

Before my first class, I duck into the bathroom, and while I'm in the stall, a few girls come in, voices I don't recognize. While I'm there, I hear a conversation that goes like:

"He's so *dreamy*. I mean, you heard what he did for Parker."

"He *totally* saved her from the Hooded Sweatshirt Stalker," says another.

I perk up at this. Are they talking about Ryan? They must be. Who else would "save" Parker?

"He even walks her to class," says another.

"I wouldn't mind him walking me to the bedroom," says another.

"Doesn't he have a girlfriend, though?"

"Yeah, but I don't know what he sees in her. I mean, *look* at her."

"She's like, *completely* flat."

"Totally."

"And I don't think she's even that pretty."

"I mean, Ryan could have any girl he wanted . . ."

Ryan. It's for certain now. There's only one Ryan at Bard that a group of three girls would be gossiping about. That's *my* Ryan. And the flat-chested girl they're talking about is *me*.

I flush, and step out of the stall, taking brief satisfaction in the shocked look on the girls' faces.

"Oh, don't stop talking on *my* account," I say. "Please, continue."

The girls, frozen to the spot, come to life all at once. They file stiff-legged out of the bathroom. Outside they burst into laughter. I roll my eyes.

Great. *Freshmen* are talking about me. Specifically, about my lack of cleavage. Don't they have anything better to do? But I don't know why I'm surprised. Since I became Ryan's girlfriend, I'm on everyone's gossip list. From what I'm wearing, to whether or not we're going to break up, everyone seems to want to talk about us. It's the downside of dating Ryan Kent. I'm surprised we don't have one of those celebrity monolithic names like Ryanda or Miran.

I check out my reflection quickly in the mirror, but don't see anything out of place, like ketchup on my face or my hair sticking up. It's just me, the reassuringly normal, middle-of-the-road Miranda. I've dyed my hair a lighter shade of brunette, a tad lighter than last semester's nearly jet-black look. I've got on Ryan's oversize letterman's jacket, which is so long it nearly reaches the hem of my skirt. But it's warm and nice, especially in February. Otherwise I'm the same. Not the prettiest girl, but certainly not the ugliest. I'm what my mom calls "approachable," which somehow always sounds like a little bit of an insult. Still, I'm not hideous. I'm worthy of Ryan Kent, even if I don't fill out a B-cup bra.

Outside the bathroom, a girl runs by and hands me a pink flyer. I expect it to be another mug shot of the Bard Campus Would-Be Rapist, but instead, it's a flyer for a dance. It says "Spring Break Dance, March 17. Help us plan! Join the Bard Pride and Spirit Committee."

"You got one of those, too?" Hana asks me, catching me in the hall on my way to theology class.

"What is the 'Bard Pride and Spirit Committee'?"

Hana frowns. "That's Parker Rodham's group. She

formed it last year and tried to convince the powers that be around here to hold a prom for seniors. Apparently she only managed to convince them to have a spring break dance, since we don't actually get a spring break around here."

"Awkward dancing was the one thing I didn't mind leaving behind in my old school."

"You know Parker. She's not happy unless she's making life a little more miserable for all of us," Hana says, sighing. "Anyway, what are you worried about? You've already got a date. You can take Ryan."

I perk up a bit. Instant Dance Date: one of the many perks of dating Ryan Kent.

"Well, you could take Samir," I counter.

"But we're just friends," Hana says, sounding appalled.

"Right. Just friends," I say, not buying it. Those two are so in denial.

"We are," Hana says, in a tone so firm that I decide to drop it. The bell rings, announcing the start of the next class.

Hana ducks into sophomore lit and I head to theology down the hall.

"Hey, *Miranda*," says Derek Mann, stepping in front of me. Derek is one of Ryan's basketball teammates and also a giant a-hole. He's a notorious mlut (man slut) and has a reputation for hitting on anything that moves.

"Derek, I'm late," I say, trying to move past him, but he moves with me, blocking my path at every turn. He holds up his notebook like it's a stop sign. He's actually written "Derek's the Mann" on it. Gross.

"Is it true about you and Ryan?" Derek asks me, leaning in and giving me a leer. His breath smells foul. I don't know how a guy scores as much as Derek is rumored to score when he's never used a Tic Tac. But then again, he's tall, broad, and athletic, and I guess some girls just don't care about fresh breath. Derek is cute in a probably-already-has-every-STD-known-to-man kind of way. He got sent to Bard because he knocked up his principal's daughter, or so the rumor goes. Apparently he got her pregnant while he already had a pregnant girlfriend. He's the K-Fed of my generation.

"That we're dating? Yeah, we are," I say.

"No, silly," Derek says, and this time he leans in and pushes a bit of hair out of my face, invading my personal space and filling it with his dragon breath. "The *other* rumor."

Does Derek Mann hang out in the girls' bathroom, too?

"I don't know what you're talking about," I say, annoyed. Is this about the other night in the woods? I don't have time to figure it out, though. I don't want a tardy because of Derek Mann. And have I mentioned the halitosis? Serious *ew.* The second bell, signaling tardiness, rings. "Now *move.* I'm late."

"Sizzle pooh," Derek says to me as I push past him. He's always making up Derek slang. "Sizzle pooh" is his way of saying "nice butt." When I look back to frown at him, I see Derek has his eyes fixed on my rear.

I have never felt so in need of a shower.

Seven

"Ms. Tate, you're late," Coach H says, accidentally rhyming and causing a couple of snickers from the stoners who sit in the back of the class. They wear their hair in their face and find everything funny.

"Sorry, I—"

"Sit!" Coach H bellows, waving his hand to show he doesn't want any excuses. I like Coach H under normal circumstances. He's sort of like a big grizzly bear. As long as you don't take his curtness personally, you realize he really does care about you.

I mean, last semester he and Ms. W saved me from Dracula, so I know he cares about me, even if he doesn't like to let on he does. The fact is, he doesn't have great people skills, and besides, Ernest Hemingway isn't known for his patience. Plus, he's stuck teaching theology, which I can tell isn't his favorite subject. He was much better suited for last semester's history class, where he could show off his World War I artifacts.

I slide into my seat, right next to Parker Rodham, and can't help but notice she's gloating. She's always happy if I get in trouble. Theology is one of several courses that's a mix of sophomores and juniors.

Like all classrooms at Bard Academy, this one is predictably dark and grim-looking. Instead of modern desks with plastic chairs, we have to sit in these old, wooden chairs with small desks attached to the arms. The desk-chairs are bolted to the ground, so you can't move them at all. Hana tells me this was because one year a student hopped up on crystal meth threw a chair through a window and tried to escape. I don't know if this is just another Campus Legend or not, but whatever. It's as good an explanation as any for why we have to sit on ancient chairs that don't move.

I glance over at Parker and notice she's wearing a button on her Bard blazer. It's got an artist's rendered drawing of the Hooded Sweatshirt Guy, and says "Catch the Stalker!" She sees me staring at her button and she leans over and whispers, "Ryan says 'hi.' "

I frown at her. She must know I haven't seen him yet today. He's probably already walked her to and from a dozen buildings by now.

"By the way, thanks for being so understanding,"

Parker continues, her voice dripping sarcasm. "I mean, other girls would get jealous about lending out their boyfriends. Especially a boyfriend like Ryan."

What she really means is: "I am so stealing your boyfriend and there's nothing you can do about it." Before I can respond, Coach H clears his throat, signaling the start of class.

Reluctantly I settle in to listen to the lecture while I try to think of ways I can kill Parker. Maybe a Bic pen to the jugular would work.

We're currently in the middle of studying the Puritans, and as in most classes at Bard, we've found a way to link it to classic literature. We've just finished reading *The Scarlet Letter,* and now we're going to start on the play *The Crucible,* both of which deal with Puritan extremism. I'm not a huge Hawthorne fan (they all made far too big a deal out of a little affair, if you ask me. I mean, Hester Prynne's husband was presumed dead, lost at sea, and she's supposed to be celibate her whole life? As far as I can tell, her only crime is not using birth control, and that wasn't exactly her fault since it was pre-Trojan times).

"First, we have business to take care of. Your papers," Coach H barks. Boy, he's in a particularly foul mood this afternoon.

He walks down the aisles of the class, handing out our papers. I thought I did an unusually good job on mine ("The Real Scarlet Letter: Puritanism in America"). Even after one semester at Bard, I've learned the importance of putting colons in your paper titles. They make you sound smarter than you are.

I've yet to break the A barrier in this class, but if any paper could do it, it's this one. I did research, I even have a bibliography; basically above and beyond the opinion essay we were supposed to write. I even made a cover sheet, which is more than I can say for most everybody else.

So it comes as quite a surprise when Coach H plops down my paper and on the cover there's a big, fat, red . . . F.

An F? How can this be? I flip to the end of the paper where it simply reads: "Plagiarism will not be tolerated. This is your one and only warning. Next time, severe disciplinary action will follow."

I glance around me as if I can find the answer in the air. I didn't plagiarize anyone! This is 100 percent my original work, such that it is. My eyes fall on Parker Rodham's desk, which is next to mine, and I see that she's got her paper faceup. It's got a bright red A on it, as well as "good work!" with an exclamation mark. And the title is . . . "The Real Scarlet Letter: Puritanism in America."

"Hey . . ." I hiss at Parker, who just looks up at me and gives me a slow, deliberate smile. She's done this on purpose. She's framed me for plagiarism. And then I remember seeing one of her clones in the library two weeks ago. The one who asked to borrow some notebook paper, the one who was sitting at the table when I got up to find a book in the stacks and bumped into Ryan, who kept me distracted for longer than I intended. I'd left my backpack there, along with the first draft of my theology paper. The clone must've copied it, replaced it, and then given a copy to Parker. That was a few days before the paper was due. I bet she gave Coach H an early draft, just to plant the seed that *she* was the one with the original work. She framed me. Evil witch!

Parker just straightens the papers on her desk and acts as if nothing is wrong. I suppose I should count myself lucky. Being framed for plagiarism is better than getting my Pellegrino spiked with rat poison, which is allegedly what she did to her own mother.

I fume until the bell rings, signaling the end of class. But as I try to present my case to Coach H, he doesn't seem to want to hear it.

"You can't really believe I copied this paper," I say. "The colon was *totally* my idea!"

"I'm sorry, Miss Tate, but Parker told me about her paper in advance. She showed me a copy."

"But Parker copied *me*. One of her friends took my paper in the library. And—"

"Miranda, I *want* to believe you," Coach H says, his

tough exterior showing a little unexpected tenderness. "And I do believe you. Because I know Parker, is well, simply put . . . lacking in scruples. But she didn't leave me much choice here. The evidence—which I'm sure is planted by her—is all on her side, and I can't play favorites."

"But—"

"Just be careful next time, and be glad I don't send you to Headmaster B, because she takes a far harder line on plagiarism than I do. She believes it's a figurative expulsion offense."

Like the Puritans in *The Scarlet Letter*, Bard faculty sometimes punish students by shunning them. Figurative expulsion is one of these shunning punishments, in which a student is ordered not to talk to or interact with any other student or faculty member for a certain amount of time. No students are allowed to talk to you, either. You wear a red sweater vest, so basically you walk around campus like a ghost, unable to talk or interact with anyone or have anyone talk to you. It's one of the worst punishments at Bard, and more feared even than toilet cleaning duty.

"But Coach, this is not fair. I didn't do this," I say, trying to keep my voice at a reasonable level, but failing. The unfairness of it is just too hard to swallow. Not to mention the fact that Parker got an A because she stole all my hard work.

"Is there a problem here?" asks Headmaster B, who appears from nowhere as she often does. She's more ghostlike than any of the teacher ghosts around here, and by far the strictest. She's only about four feet tall, but she's not someone you want to mess with.

"We were just finished here, weren't we, Ms. Tate?" Coach says, nodding his head in the direction of the exit.

"Fine," I grind out. I heave a frustrated sigh, snatch my paper off his desk, and stomp out of the room. It's not very mature, but I can't help it. It's so not fair.

Outside class, on the stairs leading out, I nearly bump straight into Ryan. He's wearing his Bard blazer open, and his tie loose. He looks good enough to eat. And, even better, Parker is nowhere to be found. For once!

Immediately some of my anger at Parker fades a little, as I take in Ryan's smile of recognition and feel the warmth of his arm as he swings it around me.

"You look like you're on the warpath," he says, his arm casually around my shoulder.

"You have no idea," I say.

"How about you tell me over lunch?"

Eight

One of the unwritten perks of having a boyfriend is that you never really have to worry about eating alone again. It's what relationships are about, really. You have a permanent, standing date for movies and meals.

I'm not sure how Ryan will react when I tell him his new charity project, Parker, has framed me. When I tell him about the plagiarism, he seems to take her side.

"I can't believe she'd do that on purpose," Ryan says, shaking his head. Ryan is not someone who likes to believe there are bad people in the world. He's sort of an eternal optimist. It's probably the result of having so many things come so easy to him. He just doesn't realize the lengths other people will go to have what he has naturally.

"She definitely did it," I say.

"Maybe it was just an honest mistake," Ryan says.

"Are you defending her?"

"Well, no, I mean, not exactly. It's just, I didn't think she'd do something like that."

I roll my eyes. Ryan has no idea what Parker is capable of. I'm sure she only shows him her Mother Teresa personality.

As we stand in line for our food, a few girls walk past us and giggle. I think for a second that they might be laughing at me, but then I quickly dismiss the idea. I should be used to Ryan's effect on girls by now. He turns even forty-year-old soccer moms into giggly little girls. He's got that kind of charisma.

"I know you find this hard to believe, but she's not as nice to other people as she is to you. You know the rumor about her and her mother."

"Look, I don't know all the details, but I do know that you can't believe everything you hear."

I find myself annoyed that Ryan keeps defending Parker. What gives?

"Yeah, like what they say about your car wreck," I say, and then immediately regret it. We haven't actually talked about Ryan's car crash, the one that sent him here a year ago. He was driving his girlfriend home and wound up wrapping his car around a telephone pole, killing her. Rumor was that Ryan may have been drinking, although it's also rumored he passed a blood-alcohol test. Ryan never brings it up at all, which I think is a little strange. At some point, you might want to confide in your girlfriend about it, or at least admit it happened. But he doesn't even acknowledge it.

Like right this second, when he abruptly changes the subject.

"They call this steak?" he says, pointing to the mushy, brown lump of meat covered in brown gravy that's shoved unceremoniously onto our dinner trays. He's dodged the issue, again. "Say, I have a surprise for you."

"You do? I hope it isn't that you know where this steak came from," I say, eyeing the food in line with some trepidation.

"It's in my blazer pocket. Go on. It's a gift."

I reach into his left pocket and pull out a small, pink drawstring bag.

"What's this?"

"Don't tell me you don't know what day it is," Ryan says. When I look blank, he says, "Happy Valentine's Day—ring a bell now?"

Valentine's! I'd totally forgotten. It's not like I'm used to having someone give me a valentine. Normally it's a holiday where I lay low and try to pretend I don't care that I don't have a boyfriend. Except this year, I *do* have a boyfriend. A boyfriend who's giving me a present! For a split second, I completely forget Parker.

"I'm guessing this means you didn't get me something," Ryan says, but he's smiling. He doesn't seem to care.

"I *totally* forgot," I say, feeling embarrassed. Not to mention guilty. I was too busy obsessing over Heathcliff to remember my own boyfriend on Valentine's Day.

"That's okay," Ryan says, shrugging. "I like that you're different from other girls, and you don't think Valentine's Day is a big deal."

I wonder if he's talking about one of his exes. Specifically, *the* ex, Rebecca, the one who died in the car wreck. I tear into the package and pull out a small silver bracelet with a heart charm.

"Ryan! I love it," I say, immediately putting it on. "Thank you."

"I'm glad," he says, and leans down and kisses my nose. This causes more giggles behind me, but I ignore them.

We take our so-called food from the line, and I can't help but think that people might be staring at us as we make our way across the cafeteria. I tell myself this isn't anything new. After all, people like to look at Ryan Kent.

We find Samir and Hana sitting in the corner and join them. They seem to be intent on some serious discussion in urgent whispers because when we come to their table, their conversation abruptly stops. Not them, too! I tell myself they were probably talking about the Bard ghosts, but for some reason that explanation just doesn't feel right to me. Something else is going on here.

"What's up, guys?" I ask them, but they both fall resolutely silent. And when I sit down, Hana won't make eye contact with me and Samir turns a dull shade of red, like he's seen me naked and doesn't want to admit it. Just what is going on around here?

"Uh, nothing," Hana says, staring at her soggy green beans.

"Where's Blade?" I ask the table.

"Over there," Samir says, nodding toward an adjacent table where Blade is sitting on the lap of Number Thirty-one, her basketball crush.

"She's dating Kinsey! No way," Ryan says, not quite believing his eyes. From the shell-shocked look on Kinsey's face, he doesn't believe it, either.

"Kinsey? Is that his name?" Hana asks Ryan.

"Well, he's sort of sex-obsessed, so we call him Kinsey. You know, after the sex scientist. I think his real name is Kilgore or something like that."

At the word "sex-obsessed," Samir clears his throat uncomfortably and Hana shifts in her seat. Just what in the world is going on around here?

Ryan scarfs down his food, even as the rest of us

pick at ours, and then he hops up and tells us that he's got basketball practice that he can't miss.

"Coach H will make me run laps if I'm late," he says, grabbing his backpack and giving me a quick, sweet peck on the cheek before he ducks out of the cafeteria.

"Okay, you two," I say, looking at them both. "Tell me what the heck is going on. What were you two talking about before we got here?"

"Do you want to tell her?" Samir asks Hana.

"No way, I don't want to tell her," Hana says, shaking her head.

"Well, *I'm* a guy, so *I* can't tell her," Samir says. "It's in the rules."

"What rules?" Hana cries.

"The ones I made up just now. Besides, you're the one who heard the rumor."

"Would *someone* just tell me what is going on?" I cry, getting frustrated.

"Okay, *fine,* I'll do it," Hana says, sighing. She looks at me. "People are saying that you wearing Ryan's jacket means that you had sex with him."

"What?" I cry. I don't add that this is impossible, since I am the big V.

"That's not all. You, uh, also had sex with the starting lineup of the basketball team," Hana says.

"Well, technically not sex. Just blow jobs."

"WHAT!" I shout, and then lower my voice when other people start to stare. "That's ridiculous."

"It's what people are saying," Samir says.

I flashback to Derek slithering up to me in the hall. No wonder he was so flirty with me, since he thought I'd partied with the entire starting lineup of the Bard Academy varsity basketball team. He must've felt left out since he's a benchwarmer, not a starter. Ugh. I think I might vomit.

"Wait, it gets worse," Hana says.

"I don't see how that's possible," I say.

"I think Parker is the one spreading the rumors," Hana says. "She's telling everyone that the reason why she returned the jacket to Ryan was because he asked her to do this and she's not 'that kind of girl.'"

Parker wore Ryan's jacket for a brief period last semester, but Ryan says he's the one who asked for it back, and he only leant it to her because she got caught in the rain and was cold. They'd never actually had a relationship, according to Ryan.

"That's a lie," I say. "She had to give back the jacket because Ryan asked for it back."

"Not according to her," Hana says.

"I don't feel so good." I put my head on the cafeteria table.

The very idea that everyone thinks I fooled around with the entire basketball team makes me really think

I might be sick. I have standards, you know. High ones. I'd only had two kisses before I went with Ryan, and now suddenly it's Miranda Does Bard?

I glance down at Ryan's letterman jacket and see the bright red B. It feels like a brand: B for bimbo.

This is it, I think. The very last straw.

I am going to have to kill Parker Rodham.

Nine

Parker Rodham, however, isn't easy to kill.

She's one of the most popular (and feared) girls on campus. Any girl not in her clique wants to be in it. And even those brave enough to say they despise her don't dare say it to her face.

"How am I supposed to get even?" I ask Hana, as the two of us watch Parker Rodham and her clones walk past us. Hana and I are standing in front of a stone statue of Shakespeare, in the middle of the campus commons. Even Shakespeare manages to look creepy on the Bard campus. He's got blank eyes, and his quill pen is raised at an odd angle. In the semidark of dusk, he looks a lot like a psycho killer, getting ready to stab someone. I only wish his victim were Parker.

"You don't, unless you want to get dead," Hana

says. "I mean, do you see any of her ex-boyfriends around?"

This is one of the nagging rumors about Parker. All of her exes seem to magically disappear the minute they break up. Most people think she poisons them.

"Does that really happen, though? I mean, she can't just kill people," I say. "Where are the bodies?"

"The river," Hana says. "Or the woods. Or the ocean. I've heard all kinds of stories."

"You think Headmaster B would really put up with Parker killing people?"

"Let's just say I don't want to find out, okay?" Hana asks.

"What are you guys talking about?" Blade asks, jumping into our conversation midstream.

"Nothing," Hana says.

"Parker Rodham," I say.

"I could put a hex on her," Blade offers. "All I'd need is a live chicken sacrifice."

"Ew!" Hana says.

"What? It would *totally* work," Blade says. "I've only tried it with Perdue frozen chicken breasts, but I *swear* a live chicken would work."

"Um, no thanks," I say.

"You coming to the pit?" Hana asks me while ignoring Blade.

The pit is a giant stone circle at the center of campus in front of the chapel. Every night there's a lit fire there, which seems like a pretty bad idea given the sheer number of serious pyromaniacs around here. But so far, no one has burned down anything (except for last year's Bard arsonist, and she wasn't technically a student). This is probably because the pit is the only place on campus whose purpose is purely social. There are stone benches around it, and it's too dark to study. The only other gathering places are the library and the dining hall, and both of them are heavily monitored by Bard faculty. The pit is monitored, too, just at more of a distance.

"I don't think I feel like it," I say. Parker will be there, her underlings having probably already scouted out the best seats, and besides, the pit is the perfect place for a ghost story. And the last thing I need at this point is a ghost story. I can still see those red eyes I saw in the forest, and I don't need anything else around here to feed my bogeyman imagination, thanks.

"Besides, I want to find Ryan," I add.

"Suit yourself," Hana says.

"I'll come," Blade offers. Hana seems less than enthused, but Blade doesn't seem bothered.

"Fine." Hana sighs, sends me a look that says "see what you've done—now I'm alone with chicken-sacrifice girl," and trudges off to the pit.

I turn and start down the path that will lead me to the gym, so I can talk to Ryan. It's starting to get dark, and I suddenly wish that Hana had tried harder to convince me to go with her. The sun has long since sunk behind the trees, and the sky looks pink and blue at once. The lamps along the path flicker on while I walk, giving everything a kind of creepy glow. Even the icicles in the trees cast weird shadows on the ground. It's so cold, my breath comes out in white puffs.

I don't want to talk to Ryan about the rumors, but I don't see that I have a choice, either. He's the only one who can make this right.

Up ahead, I see a dark figure standing near the gym. At first, I think it might be a Guardian, but then I realize it's someone else.

In fact, it's the Hooded Sweatshirt Stalker. And he's fifteen feet from me.

He turns slightly, but it's too dark for me to see his face. He sees me and he pauses a second.

"Heathcliff?" I whisper, although he's too far away to hear me. I stop in my tracks, as if worried that any sudden movement will send him running off to the woods. I try to glimpse his face, but I can't. The size and shape of him could be Heathcliff, but then again, it could also be someone who has the same build.

Before I can decide for sure, he takes off at a sharp

angle off the path at a trot. I run after him, but it's no use. He's faster, and it's dark, and he's into the woods before I even cover half the distance between us.

I can't help but wonder, if it is Heathcliff why won't he talk to me?

On the path to the gym, where he'd been standing, I find another scrap of paper on the ground. It looks like another piece of the same drawing I found the other week. Absentmindedly I put my hand into my Bard blazer. Sure enough, the piece is still there. I'd totally forgotten about it. I take it out and the pieces fit together. It's definitely an ear, and an eye. It could be a cat, I think. Strange. Why do I always find these in the wake of the Hooded Sweatshirt Stalker? I put the two pieces of paper back in my pocket, as I swing open the gym doors and go in.

I find Ryan inside. He's shooting hoops with Derek Mann, which makes me cringe. As I approach, Derek gives me a leer, making me want to go take a shower.

"Miranda!" Ryan cries, surprised.

"Can I talk to you . . . alone?" I ask, looking at Derek.

"Whatever you have to say in front of Ryan, you can say in front of me, sweetheart," Derek says.

"Mann, come on." Ryan gives Derek a playful shove.

"Anyway, practice is going to start soon," Derek says.

"I don't think Coach H is showing up. He's never late, and it's fifteen past," Ryan says. He tosses Derek the ball. "Come on, Miranda. Let's go."

I fall into step beside him.

"Coach H skipped a practice?" I ask Ryan. "That's not like him. He lives for sports."

"I know, it's kind of weird. Maybe he's sick or something," Ryan says.

"Yeah, maybe," I say, not adding that ghosts don't get sick.

"Did you walk here alone? You know it's not safe."

I shrug.

"You shouldn't have done that," Ryan says. "Parker really thinks this guy is for real. She really thought he was going to hurt her."

"I know, but . . . about Parker," I start. And then stop.

Yeah. This is the hard part. I'm not sure exactly how to tell Ryan about the rumor, and my face is bright red just thinking about putting it into words. This is worse than fifth-grade sex education when I was called upon to answer the question "What is a testicle?"

I decide the best approach is a direct one.

"Parker Rodham is spreading the rumor that I had to do you and the whole basketball team as a condition of wearing this jacket," I blurt out at once.

Ryan stops in his tracks, looks at me, then bursts out laughing.

"This isn't funny!" I say.

"It is kind of funny," Ryan says. "Who would believe that?"

I'm temporarily relieved that Ryan has such faith in the power of my reputation as a good girl. "Derek Mann, for one. And lots of others," I say.

"Well, that's just stupid," Ryan says.

"I know it's stupid and you know it's stupid, but everyone else thinks it really happened," I say.

"If people want to make stories up, who cares? We know it isn't true."

"But you have to say something. People are talking about me in restrooms. It's got to stop."

Ryan gives me a puzzled look.

"What am I supposed to do? Stand up at morning assembly and announce that I haven't laid a finger on you? And that you haven't, as rumored, slept with the basketball team?"

"That would be a good start."

"Miranda," Ryan says, exhaling a frustrated sigh. "You can't be so concerned about what other people think. People who are envious of what we have are going to spread rumors. If you start to let them get to you, then you're only going to make yourself unhappy. If I stop this rumor, there will just be another one, sooner or later. That's how people work. You just have to ignore them."

"This is pretty hard to ignore. Derek nearly assaulted me in the hall," I say.

"He *what*?" Ryan cries, and now I suddenly have his attention.

"He thought the rumor was an open invitation," I add.

Ryan's mouth settles into a thin line. "I'll take care of him," Ryan says. "Okay?"

"Okay." I feel a little better. Still, I can't shake a minor annoyance. Why isn't Ryan as upset about this as I am? He seems to take it all in stride. Then again, he is a boy. Having a rumor about how you can get girls to do your sexual bidding for the privilege of wearing your jacket doesn't exactly reflect badly on him. Instantly I banish that thought. Ryan isn't that kind of guy. He's a good guy. A nice one. Isn't he?

"Come on, let's not let a dumb rumor spoil our evening," Ryan says, sliding his arm around my waist and tugging me closer. "Hey, let's go to the pit. We've still got half an hour till underclassmen curfew."

I guess he's right. I shouldn't let Parker spoil *all* my fun.

"Lead the way," I tell him.

Unfortunately we don't make it two steps outside the gym before we run straight into Parker Rodham.

Speak of the devil, and she'll crash your hot date. As if I should be surprised.

"Do you guys know it's almost curfew?" she says in a singsong voice, as she puts herself between me and Ryan, and Ryan's arm falls away from my shoulders to let her in.

"We have nearly a half hour," I say, but Parker ignores me.

"I didn't want you to get in trouble, Ryan," she says, laying a possessive hand on his arm. She doesn't even acknowledge me and I'm standing inches from her.

"Um, thanks, Parker," Ryan says.

"Am I interrupting anything?" Parker asks, when she clearly already knows the answer to that question. "I mean, I was going to go to the pit, but I hate walking alone. With that *rapist* out there. Do you think you could walk with me?" She hangs on Ryan's arm, still ignoring me.

"You made it this far by yourself," I say, but she continues to ignore me. Ryan, however, chuckles, and then quickly swallows the laugh when he sees how earnest Parker is being.

"I was nearly killed," Parker says, her face somber.

Ryan immediately looks sympathetic. "Sorry," he says.

I roll my eyes. Sometimes Ryan is far too gullible.

The three of us start walking, and Parker has effectively staked out the territory between me and Ryan. As we walk, Parker loops her arm through Ryan's possessively.

"I'm cold," she explains, cuddling up to him. I don't think I can take much more of this. Seriously. "And didn't Miranda see something in the woods? A monster, I heard someone say."

Parker gives me one of her most innocent-looking evil smiles.

Ryan gives me a funny, sidelong glance. Did Ryan *tell* her? Ryan told her I'd seen something in the woods? How could he *do* that?

"I never said it was a monster," I say, feeling a bit betrayed. Ryan looks a little sheepish. He mouths to me "sorry." He *did* tell her. I could kill him.

"That's not what I heard. I heard you thought it was going to eat you."

"I saw a big animal, that's all."

"Where did you see it?" Parker asks. "Wasn't it near here somewhere?" Her voice sends a chill down my spine. She knows I don't want to go anywhere near the woods. Who would? It's pitch-black, and I'm not nearly as dumb as I was when I first got here. I know there are things *living* in the woods. Big things. With fangs. Parker takes a step closer to the woods. "Why don't you show us?"

"It's too dark to see now," I say.

"What are you? Afraid?" Parker taunts. Right now, I really, *really* hate her. What are we? Ten?

I should let her taunts roll off me, but I can't. I don't like being told I'm afraid in front of Ryan. It doesn't seem right. Besides, he already thinks the whole thing is a big joke. He didn't see the glowing red eyes. He doesn't know about half the things that go on around here. Neither does Parker.

"I can show you, but it won't make a difference," I say.

"It's too dark anyway," Ryan says, trying to save me. "Let's save it."

"No," Parker says. Her voice is steely and resolved. "I want to see it now. I want Miranda to show us."

I glare at Parker and she glares back. She knows she has me. She's not going to let this go.

"Fine," I say. I walk off the lighted path toward the woods. I stop about ten feet from them. "It was about there," I say, pointing to the old oak tree where I saw the animal.

"Here?" Parker says, stepping in front of me. She walks boldly up to the tree. "Right here?"

"About there."

"So why don't you come over here? Are you scared to be close to the tree?" she says, and touches it with one hand.

"I'm not scared," I snap, but I sound like a kinder-garten. "This is childish," I add, before walking over to the tree and standing by Parker. "There? Are you happy now?"

Then, deep in the woods we hear a wolf's howl. I glance quickly in the direction of the sound, but Parker just looks at me and laughs. "Do you sleep with the light on, too?"

"Why don't we go inside?" Ryan says, glancing at me with a worried look on his face. I can't tell if he thinks I'm a total idiot or if he's uncomfortable that I'm uncomfortable.

"How much would you pay me, Miranda, to walk five feet into the woods right now?"

"I wouldn't pay you anything, Parker."

"What if I paid you one hundred dollars to do it. Would you?"

"Parker, quit fooling around. Let's go inside." Ryan sounds less patient now.

"What? I'm just saying. Look," she says. She walks into the woods and is quickly enveloped in shadow. We hear her footsteps in the leaves and then, sud-denly, they stop.

I glance over at Ryan, and he looks over at me.

"Why don't we just leave her in there?" I whisper to him. He laughs.

"Parker?" Ryan calls. "Parker, come on." She doesn't

answer. Ryan tries again. "Parker! Seriously. Quit it. Come on."

Still no answer.

"Parker. Come out, already. We're cold," Ryan says.

I have that eerie feeling. You know the one. Like Parker's been slashed into a million pieces by some chain saw–wielding maniac or a monster with red eyes, and we're next.

"Parker?"

The next thing we hear is a scream.

Ten

Ryan leaps into the woods, because he is ridiculously brave *and* good-looking. He is so going to be a firefighter one of these days. I go in after him, not because I want to save Parker, but because I really don't want to be left alone.

We only make it a step or two before Parker nearly collides with us. She has something dark and sticky on her hands.

Blood.

She's mumbling inconsolably, pointing backward. That's when the clouds covering the moon lift and it suddenly gets brighter. There, lying only five feet away, is the carcass of a dead bear. Its mouth is open, and its tongue is out, and it has a big bloody gash down the side of its neck.

Instantly I think of the creature with red eyes I saw in the woods. Could it have done this? I shiver.

I look at Parker and realize she must've tripped over the bear, or fallen into it. She's got bear blood on her hands and a big dark smear down the front of her white Bard shirt.

She buries her face in Ryan's chest, and he folds his arms around her to comfort her. My stomach shrinks, and not because of the dead bear. I don't like Ryan hugging Parker.

"Come on," he says. "Let's get out of here."

The next morning, everyone is talking about Parker's run-in with the bear. I've about decided that it doesn't matter *what* Parker does. People will still want to talk about it anyway. I can just see the next *Bard Weekly* headline: "Parker Pops Zit, Entire Campus Watches."

"Don't look now, but Parker has co-opted your boyfriend again," Hana says, nodding in the direction of Parker and Ryan, who are standing in a group of Parker's clones and relating the bear story. "I have a feeling we're going to be hearing about this all day."

"Did you hear about the bear?" Blade asks me, finding us in line. Hana rolls her eyes.

"Duh—Miranda was there."

"Really? Why don't you *tell* me these things?"

"I would've, if you'd been *awake."* Blade was fast asleep when I got back to my dorm. And that was at eight o'clock.

"So did Ryan kill the bear with his bare hands like they say?" Blade asks as we take our seats at a table near Parker's. I try to get Ryan's attention, but he's too busy pantomiming the act of saving Parker from a bear carcass. I'm still peeved he told Parker about my monster sighting. How could he have betrayed my trust like that? *And* to Parker, of all people?

"No. The bear was already dead."

"Was the bear big? I heard it was five hundred pounds."

"It was huge," I say. "But what we should worry about is whatever killed that bear. I don't think it was a hunter. The bear was half-eaten."

"Ew!" Hana says. "I'm trying to eat my breakfast slop here."

"Guys! Bear? Did you hear?" Samir says, joining us as he slides his tray down in front of an empty chair.

"Duh—old news!" Blade says, waving her hand as if she hadn't just heard the story five minutes ago. "So do you think that bear was killed by that monster you saw in the woods?"

"What did you see in the woods?" Hana asks me.

"If you tell me Dracula, I am so going to get a transfer," Samir adds.

I guess I forgot to mention the red-eyed thing to Hana and Samir. I relate the story.

"Maybe it was just an owl," Samir suggests. "Owls are way creepy."

"They don't have glowing red eyes, dummy," Blade says, tossing her empty milk carton at him.

"And they're not big enough to kill bears," Hana adds.

"Can't blame a guy for trying to explain things logically," Samir says. "By the way, did you hear—"

"No, Parker was not bitten by anything, and *no,* Parker did not vanquish the bear by farting or whatever it is she's supposed to have done," Hana says, exasperated. "Now can I finish eating?"

"Parker farts?" Samir echoes, looking puzzled. "Anyway, what I was *going* to say is that Coach H is missing."

"He's what?"

"He was AWOL at basketball practice and for his afternoon classes yesterday, too," Samir says.

"That's weird," I say.

"Yeah. Apparently Headmaster B is going to make some kind of announcement at morning assembly."

The official excuse for Coach H's abrupt departure, according to Headmaster B, is that he's just on a leave of absence, but the four of us know that ghosts don't just take vacations. And Hana thinks whatever happened to Coach H wasn't planned in advance.

"Otherwise he would've had a substitute teacher," she points out as we file out of the chapel after morning assembly.

"Something bad happened to him, I know it," Blade says. "This is why we need to form the LITs."

"Not the club again," Hana says, exhaling a sigh.

"Maybe he escaped purgatory somehow," Samir says. "Wasn't he supposed to help people patch up bad relationships? Maybe he's done that and moved on."

"Coach H? Are we talking about the same person?" I say. Coach has a long way to go in the people skills department. "I think it might take him a long time to get out of purgatory."

"That's exactly my point," Blade says. "Something bad happened to him. We ought to investigate."

"How are we supposed to do that?" Hana asks.

"How else? Snoop around," Blade says.

Eleven

Blade's idea of snooping involves sneaking into the boys' dorm after curfew, armed with nothing more than a book of her Wiccan spells.

"I can't *believe* I let you talk me into this," I whisper as we're standing in the hallway of Macduff dorm. The dorm hallway is nearly dark, except for small lights near the floorboards. The living room is dark, and giant shadows in the corners are either sofas or bear-eating monsters. Okay, so they're probably not monsters.

Still, I'd rather not find out. I wouldn't be here at all, except for the fact that Blade guilt-tripped me. Coach H did save our hides last semester a couple of times when Emily Brontë was on the loose wreaking havoc. She reminded me that despite my recent falling out with Coach H, we had history, and the least I could do was try to find out what happened to him. And she's right. I only wish she could've been right during daylight hours.

"I should've listened to Hana," I say and sigh.

Hana was, at this moment, sleeping in her bed back in our dorm, where we were supposed to be. She was having no part in snooping. She said the idea was stupid, and not worth the risk of dish duty—our punishment should Guardians catch us breaking curfew.

"Where's your sense of adventure?" Samir asks me. He's the one who let us into the dorm.

"As if you have a single adventurous bone in your body," I whisper back. Samir is the biggest coward I know.

"I ate the foul goopy stuff they called dinner. That's the very *definition* of adventurous."

"Shhhhhhhhh," Blade hisses at us. A light at the end of the hall comes on, sending us all scurrying to find hiding spots.

I duck behind one of the giant shadows—a couch, thankfully. Blade flattens herself against a bookcase, and Samir, caught without a place to hide, simply stands in the corner of the room near the fireplace with his chin jutting out, like some kind of pajama-wearing statue.

The light flicks off, but then a flashlight beam bounces along the floor. It's being wielded by a Guardian, who is patrolling the halls, looking for curfew breakers. He must not be looking very hard, because he passes by the living room with only a cursory look, managing to miss Samir, who is standing in the corner with his hand inside his pajama lapel like he's imitating Napoleon.

After the Guardian disappears around the corner, I let out the breath I didn't realize I'd been holding.

"A statue?" Blade hisses at Samir, sounding disapproving.

"What? It worked for Shaggy on *Scooby-Doo*."

The three of us move down the hall—in the opposite direction of the Guardian—toward Coach H's room.

The door is locked.

Blade whips out what looks like a Swiss army knife and proceeds to pick the lock.

"How did you learn how to do that?" I ask her. "Is that in your Wicca training?"

"No, you dummy. I got busted for breaking and entering. I picked our neighbor's garage and stole their set of lawn gnomes."

"*That's* why you got sent here?" Samir asks. "Lawn gnomes? You have to be kidding."

Blade shrugs. "That and my dad is a pastor. He thinks pagan worship is the devil's work."

"Wait. Rewind. Your *dad* is a pastor?" Samir can't believe his ears. Neither can I.

"I'm going to guess that your Satan poster didn't go over really well with him," I say.

"Definitely not. He thought I might be possessed by demons," she said. "Anyway, are we going to snoop, or what?" Blade asks, pushing open the door. She lights her mini skull lighter, which casts a flickering glow to parts of the room.

Coach H's room looks normal. No papers are out of place. There's nothing that would suggest a struggle. Like all teachers' rooms, his doesn't have a bed. Ghosts don't need to sleep.

"So what are we snooping for exactly?" I ask Blade.

She gives an exasperated sigh. "*Clues*," she breathes, as if it's obvious. I'm not sure how she expects us to find them. I can barely see two feet in front of me. Straight ahead, there's a window, and it shows a perfect full moon hanging above the tree line. We're on the first floor, so the window also has a view of the chapel, about fifty feet away. The moon outside makes it look brighter out there than it is in here. While I'm considering this irony, a big black shadow moves quickly across the window.

"Did you guys see that?" I ask Samir and Blade.

"See what?" Samir asks, suddenly sounding nervous. I was wondering how long his fake-bravery act was going to last.

I look up at the window, but there's nothing there.

Maybe I just imagined it. Like you imagined the red eyes in the woods? a voice in my head tells me. Against my better judgment, I take a few steps closer to the window to get a better look. If I were in a horror movie, this is the point where you'd tell me I was an idiot for putting my nose up against the glass when something most definitely is going to jump up suddenly and scare the bejesus out of me. But this isn't a horror movie. At least, not that I know of.

I put my hand on the desk to peer out the window, and that's when I feel a bit of paper. It's the only thing on the desk and it sticks to my finger. When I inspect it, I see that it's about the size of a quarter, and it looks like another ripped piece of paper, like the one I found outside the gym and on the path near the commons. It's too dark to see exactly what the piece is, but I'm pretty sure it's part of the same picture. Before I can compare it to the other two bits, it dawns on me that this is Hooded Sweatshirt Stalker's calling card. He was here at some point. And if he was here, in Coach H's room, maybe he *did* have something to do with Coach H's disappearance.

And then, suddenly to my right, the entire wall seems to move. It's only belatedly that I realize the big shadow next to me isn't the bureau I thought it was. It's a man. A big, brawny guy. In a hooded sweatshirt.

"Ack" is the only sound I can manage as I jump

back from the figure. Part of my brain tells me it's Heathcliff and I have nothing to be afraid of, but the other, louder part of my brain says Hooded Sweatshirt Stalker could plan to hack me to pieces. He did something to Coach H, and he could do something to me.

"What the hell . . .?" Blade starts, whipping her head around and seeing Hooded Sweatshirt Guy.

It's too dark to see his face, but the stalker turns and looks at me, then at Blade and Samir, and then bolts straight out of the room. I try to follow, my legs coming to life a few seconds too late. By the time I get my feet moving, I nearly collide straight into Mr. B, who reaches into Hemingway's room and flicks on the light.

"The Hooded Sweatshirt Stalker," Blade says. "He just went that way. Did you see him?"

Blake eyes me, then Blade and Samir.

"I didn't see anyone," he says.

"But he was right there," Blade sputters.

"Yes, well," Blake adds, clearing his throat. "He's not here now. Are you trying to tell me you're out, after curfew, searching through the room of a faculty member because you're trying to trap the campus stalker?"

"Well, uh, no," Blade says.

"Did you students find what you were looking for?" he asks us calmly.

For a full minute, we're entirely silent. We've been busted by Blake, the teacher on campus voted most likely to have run out of his antipsychotic drug prescription, because of his habit of seeing things that aren't there. Unfortunately he does see us.

"Um . . . we were just, uh . . ." Blade stammers, desperately trying to think of an excuse.

"We were looking for our homework assignment," I say. Okay, so this is totally lame. But it's better than "we were snooping around pretending to be Veronica Mars because Blade has this idea that we should form a mystery society."

"Yes, right, well then," Blake says, clearly not believing us. "I'm not certain, but I believe you all have beds to go to."

"You're not punishing us?" Samir says, bubbling to life next to me. Blade promptly kicks Samir in the shin and gives him a look that says, "thanks for reminding Blake of his options."

"No, I'm not going to punish you," Blake says. "But I suggest you get back to your rooms as soon as you can. I'm sure our friends the Guardians won't be so lenient."

He doesn't need to tell us twice. In seconds, the three of us scatter.

"What the hell was the stalker doing in Coach H's room?" hisses Blade as we trot back to our room.

"I dunno," I say, but now I'm really not so sure it's Heathcliff. I'm not so sure at all.

That night, I drift into a fitful sleep, where I'm running through the woods, lost, looking for something, and it's only middream that I realize I'm looking for Heathcliff. In the woods, I find that church by the river. In front of it, there's a big boulder and that tree again—the one that's shaped like a horseshoe.

And inside, I hear Heathcliff calling me.

I wake in a kind of panic, my heart racing. Why am I dreaming of Heathcliff nearly every night? And what does the church or the horseshoe-shaped tree mean?

"Maybe it's your lucky tree," Hana suggests at morning assembly.

"I don't know, but I think the dream is telling me Heathcliff is in trouble," I say.

"How can he be in trouble? He's back in *Wuthering Heights*," Hana says as she looks straight ahead and pretends to be listening to Headmaster B give morning announcements. She turns and looks at me. "Isn't he?"

"Right," I lie, feeling suddenly uncomfortable. I *should* tell Hana the truth, I know. I just don't know how.

"Anyway, maybe it's just the stalker stories that

are getting to you," Hana says. "Is it true about last night? Samir said you guys *saw* the stalker—up close and personal."

"Yeah, for about two seconds, then he bolted."

"Still, creepy," Hana adds. "And all this time I thought Parker was just making him up."

"Yeah, weird, huh?" I say, just as a Guardian to our right shushes us.

With only three hours of sleep after our little snooping adventure, I pretty much bomb my geometry test, and manage to walk through the rest of my morning classes like a zombie. This is the last time I let Blade talk me into anything.

I'm still feeling a little out of it by the time my counseling session with Ms. W rolls around, but at least maybe she'll have some answers. I want to tell her about the stalker, and about finding him in Coach H's room. I can't shake the feeling the two are linked somehow.

But Ms. W seems even more distracted than I am during our session. I try to talk about how we snooped around Coach H's room and about the stalker, but I get the distinct impression that she's not even listening.

I decide to test her.

"So," I say, as she glances off into space, "my dad sent in that permission form. He's so happy with my progress here at Bard that he's going to buy me a brand-new Maserati."

When Ms. W doesn't react, I know I've got her.

"Um, *hello*? Ms. Woolf?"

"Ms. W," she corrects absently. The teachers here don't like to go by their real names, since they're famous ones. Not that most of the Bard students would pick up on them anyway. Most of them aren't exactly voracious readers.

"Are you even listening?" I ask her. For once, I'm in the mood to talk about real problems and Ms. W isn't paying attention.

"Sorry, Miranda," Ms. W says, shaking her head. "I'm a little distracted. We're all a bit worried about Coach H."

"So something is up then?" I ask.

"What do you mean? What have you heard? Do you know something you're not telling me?"

"Whoa," I say, holding up my hands. "I don't know anything. Blade suspects foul play. Do you?"

"I don't know what to think. You're sure you didn't have anything to do with Coach H's disappearance?"

"Me? No! Why?"

"And you haven't been near the vault, have you?"

"No. Now what's going on?"

Ms. W hesitates, as if not sure she wants to confide in me.

"Coach H's book is missing from the vault. And some faculty suspects you may have taken it."

"Me? Why?"

"So you could trap Coach H because of the F he gave you," Ms. W adds, looking down at her lap. "I don't think it's true, but it's hard to convince the others . . ."

"What! But how does everyone know?"

"Plagiarism must be reported to the entire staff," Ms. W says. "It's Bard policy."

"Okay, but I'd never do anything like that. Is this just about me and my friends knowing about the vault? Because you can trust us, really."

"I know that, but some of the other faculty have reservations about you in particular."

"Why?"

"To be honest, they don't trust you. Because of your, uh, fictional roots. Few faculty members feel fictional characters can be trusted. Especially a descendent of Catherine Earnshaw. Who could be willful, and possibly, selfish."

"But I'm not Catherine Earnshaw. I'm Miranda Tate. We're two different people."

"I know that, and you know that, but the others . . . well, they aren't so easily convinced. You have a motive, Miranda. And the means."

"I've never been near the vault since last semester. I don't even know how to open it!"

"Just be careful. They're looking for a reason to come after you. The only reason they haven't is because they can't prove you were in the vault. But Coach H's disappearance is very serious. It's scared a lot of us, and we're not sure what to do. I could get into trouble just by telling you this."

"I understand," I say, appreciating Ms. W's trust in me. "What do you think happened to Coach H?"

Ms. W gets a faraway look in her eye. "I don't know, but some souls can't make it," Ms. W says. "He might have decided to end it."

"End it? Like suicide? But he's a ghost. How is that possible?"

"There are ways," Ms. W says, mysteriously. "Anyway, that's our time for today."

I stand up and Ms. W catches my arm. "Miranda, there's one more thing . . ." she starts. "It's about your future here at Bard."

"Yes?" I ask her.

She looks at me and then hesitates. It seems there's something she wants to tell me, but decides not to.

"Just watch yourself, okay? Because people are watching you."

Twelve

After my talk with Ms. W, I'm beginning to feel like everyone is watching me. I'm becoming extremely paranoid, and it doesn't help when I walk into theology and see that Coach's H's replacement is none other than Blake, the very teacher who caught us snooping around Coach H's room.

Nothing about this is good. Is he going to turn me in? Or has he been assigned to keep a closer eye on me?

For the first part of class, my stomach is in knots, waiting to see what he's going to do. But he doesn't do anything.

Well, nothing, that is, except spending most of the class talking to his invisible friend "Gabriele." Just like Mr. Garrison's hand puppet on *South Park*. Wow, Blade was right. This guy *is* crazy.

I can't tell if he's seriously hallucinating or if he's

just using "Gabriele" (he calls him "one of the Lord's angels") as a teaching tool. Either way, he does have a magnetism and charisma that keeps most of the class interested. That's not easy with a group of delinquents. But I suppose, given the high rates of past drug use among the Bard student body, they have a healthy respect for the bad drug trip.

"Ms. Tate," Blake says to me suddenly, his eyes brightly, lit with a fire that's usually reserved for people with fevers or psychological problems. "Gabriele would like to know why *you* think chastity was so important to the Puritans."

There are a few snickers in the class. Great. It figures I'd get the chastity question.

"They were trying to live sin-free lives, according to their beliefs in the New Testament and Calvinism," I say.

At "sin-free," other people laugh. I am really trying to be a bigger person here, but it's *really* getting difficult.

"But Gabriele says they believed in predestination, which means that God had already decided who goes to heaven and who goes to hell. So why try to lead a pious life?"

Blake has me there. I really don't know.

Before I can answer, a Goth girl in the back raises her hand. Blake nods in her direction.

"Because no one knew for *sure* if they were predestined for heaven, *duh*," she says. "Only God knows for sure."

"Very good, Ms. Kelly," Blake says. "Now, for everyone else, Gabriele has assigned you some homework. Why, if God is omnipotent, does he allow the devil to exist? And *does* the devil exist? Eight pages. By the end of the week."

There are groans around the classroom.

"Gabriele doesn't like pouters," Blake says, giving us all a look. He settles on me last. "God is watching you all. No cheating. Gabriele will know."

"I think he means you," Parker says, leaning over and whispering into my ear just as the bell rings, signaling the end of class. She's so close to me that I'm surrounded by the scent of some expensive perfume. Parker always smells like she rolled in a few issues of *Vogue*.

"By the way," she adds as I'm packing up my backpack, "did you know that today was the anniversary of Ryan's accident?"

My head whips up. It is? "How did you know about that?"

"You know I knew Rebecca," Parker says. "Our families both had summer houses at Lake Geneva. We were the best of friends."

Unfortunately, I did know this. Parker has told me many times.

"Ryan was so devastated after she died," Parker continues. "You know, I think it's why he's in this mlut phase, honestly. He was so in love with her. He used to call me all the time to talk about her, after the accident."

"He talked to you about it?" I sputter without meaning to. I've given away too much. I've literally just admitted to Parker that Ryan hasn't talked to me about the accident.

Parker's lips curl up in a gloating smile. "I wonder why he hasn't talked to you about it," she muses. "Maybe he's afraid to tell you that you don't measure up."

I'm so mad now that I'm pretty sure steam is coming out of my ears. I have a sudden urge to smash Parker's face in with my theology book.

"Anyway, Ryan might be late to dinner. He's got to walk me to cheerleading practice," she continues. "But I'm sure you won't mind."

"No—of course not," I say, my voice dripping sarcasm. "But by the way, if you *do* see Ryan today, you might want to know that he hates your cheap perfume. He told me so."

"It's not cheap! It's Chanel," Parker exclaims, sounding indignant.

"Really? Because it smells like a department store farted in here," I say as I cough and wave my hand.

"Snap! You didn't!" cries Samir in an exaggerated voice when I tell him, Hana, and Blade about my conversation with Parker. The four of us are sitting in study hall in the library.

"Sounds like you got her good," Blade agrees, a little smile on her face. "I only wish I was there to see it."

"You realize that you've now declared war on Parker," Hana says. "I don't think anyone who's ever dared insult her actually lived to tell about it for long."

"Maybe you should go into the witness protection program," Samir suggests.

"She's not going to kill you," Blade scoffs, then hesitates. "At least, probably not until after midterms."

"Thanks, guys. You are totally filling me with confidence here."

"Don't listen to them," Blade says. "I think it's great. You finally stood up for the rest of us."

"I don't feel so great," I say. "My day has gone from bad to worse. First, my boyfriend is Parker's permanent sidekick, and now I have to worry about Blake in theology. He's nuttier than a fruitcake."

"I told you guys," Blade says, "he once taught one of our entire classes while speaking in tongues."

"It doesn't surprise me. When he was alive, Blake claimed to see angels all the time," Hana explains.

"He was, and I guess is, even after death, a deeply religious man. His two major books of poetry, *Songs of Innocence* and *Songs of Experience*, deal directly with God and Christianity."

"Then why wasn't he teaching theology instead of Coach H? Coach H isn't even religious," Samir says.

"Maybe that's the point," Blade says. "Isn't that why Mary Shelley is teaching chemistry? Which, by the way, she is *terrible* at? You know, because God has a sense of irony?"

"You think God is making the teaching assignments around here?" Hana asks, skeptical. "I think that's the headmaster's job. Anyway, do you even believe in God?"

"Well, duh, of course," Blade says. "I mean, isn't this purgatory proof that He exists? We're walking with ghosts here—literally."

A Goth girl who walks by gives Blade a strange look.

"Keep your voice down," Hana whispers. "We don't want the whole school to know."

"More importantly," Blade says, lowering her voice, "what are we going to do about finding Coach H?"

"What if there's nothing to find?" I ask.

"And why do *we* have to be the detectives?" Samir whines. "Why can't we just let Ms. W figure it out?"

"Because we're the LITs," Blade says. "That's our *job*."

"I don't remember actually agreeing to be part of the LITs," Hana says.

Blade shrugs, as if that's a minor technicality. "The important thing is that Coach H needs our help."

Hana sighs. "Well, if we're going to take this seriously, we ought to start by looking for the book. If we find that, I bet we find him."

Looking for a book that someone doesn't want us to find is not as easy as it sounds. In other words, it's impossible. It's not like it's going to be filed under H for Hemingway in the school library.

Samir and Hana decide to go interview people who may have seen Coach H the day he disappeared to see if they can come up with any clues. Blade wants to go into the vault, which I think is a bad idea on a number of counts, namely because the last time we were there, Emily Brontë's ghost tried to use me to open a portal to the fictional world, which would destroy this one. Plus, digging around in the vault wouldn't be a good idea given that I'm under a cloud of suspicion with the faculty as it is. Besides, I promised Ms. W I wouldn't go near the vault, and I don't plan on breaking that promise.

* * *

"Earth to Miranda," says Ryan over dinner that night. Clearly I seem a bit distracted.

"Sorry, I'm just . . ." I try to think about what to tell Ryan. As far as he knows, Coach H is just on a simple leave of absence. I can't exactly tell him otherwise without cluing him into the real state of affairs around here. "Is it, uh, true? Is today the anniversary of your . . . accident?"

Ryan's eyes grow guarded. "Who told you that?"

"Parker," I say. "She said that you and she knew each other before Bard. And you talk to her about Rebecca."

Ryan blanches. It's probably because I rarely say Rebecca's name. His reaction, however, seems to prove what Parker said is true. He *does* talk about Rebecca with her.

"Parker talks about her," Ryan says, not actually saying the name "Rebecca." "I just listen."

"Why don't you talk about her, or the accident, with me?"

Now Ryan looks *very* uncomfortable. "It's just not something I want to talk about, okay?"

"But Parker makes it sound like . . ." I stop short before I actually say that I don't measure up to Rebecca. "Like you aren't over Rebecca."

"I am," Ryan says, sounding firm.

"But . . . she thinks that I . . ." I just can't seem to stop playing with this scab.

"That you don't compare to Rebecca?" Ryan finishes.

"Yeah. I mean, that's what Parker says."

"Well, don't listen to her," Ryan says, sounding grumpy. "And you are *nothing* like Rebecca, and did it ever occur to you that's a good thing?"

No, it didn't. Since when is being gorgeous a bad thing? And what does he mean "*nothing* like Rebecca"? Rebecca was pretty, popular, and apparently rich. I mean, I'm not rich or particularly popular, but is he saying I'm ugly?

"Am I supposed to take that as a compliment?"

"Yes. Now can we talk about something else?" Ryan's lips form a thin line.

"But . . ."

"Miranda," Ryan says, in a tone leaving no room for argument. "I don't want to talk about Rebecca. Ever. Okay?"

"Fine," I say, throwing my hands up to show surrender. Still, I feel a bit uneasy. I can't help but wonder if the rumors *are* true. Was he drunk driving, even though he passed a Breathalyzer test? And then I stop myself. I'm the victim of the gossip mill, and now suddenly I believe some rumors might be true?

"So why don't we talk about why you told Parker about what I saw in the woods?"

Ryan's eyes get bigger.

"I didn't mean to, I swear. It was an accident. It just popped out. She was asking about you, and it just kind of came out."

"Great," I say. "And do you *really* think it's necessary to follow her around all day? She sees you more than I do."

"I know, I know, and I'm sorry," Ryan says. "But . . ." Before he can finish his sentence, a freshman comes running into the cafeteria, slamming open the doors and grabbing everyone's attention.

"Monster!" the freshman shouts, and it's then that I realize his Bard uniform is missing a sleeve, like it was torn straight off, and he seems to have cuts on his face, like he was running through the forest. "There's something out there. And it nearly killed me. We've go to get out of here, before it gets us all!"

Thirteen

The entire cafeteria goes stock-still and quiet. This is saying something for a school of delinquents, where most of them have been arrested at least once. But there's something about the wild-eyed look of the freshman. He doesn't appear like he's drugged or drunk. He seems like he's telling the truth.

"You've got to help me!" he shouts, even as he goes from table to table. "There is *something* out there!"

My stomach jumps. Is he talking about the thing I saw in the woods? The red eyes? Did he see it, too?

"It was horrible . . . it was going to eat me. I swear. You have to believe me!" he rants, even as two beefy Guardians stalk toward him. The two of them grab his arms easily and lift him away from the crowd. He keeps shouting, even as the Guardians drag him through the doors of the cafeteria.

"Help me! You have to help me! There's something out there. There's something—" The cafeteria doors clang shut on his words.

For a second there's silence, and then slowly, whispers start at each of the tables, and then, almost as if on cue, the voices get louder, as if everyone is trying to compensate for the creepiness of the freshman's rant by talking at high volumes. There's laughter, almost forced laughter, from some of the tables. No matter how everyone tries to act normally, I know that most of the people are shaken. Just like me.

"Wow, what was that about?" Ryan says finally.

"I don't know," I say, watching the doors where the freshman was taken, wondering if he's all right.

"Do you think . . .?" Ryan starts, then trails off.

"Think what?" I ask him.

"No, it's stupid," Ryan says.

"No, what?" I ask him.

"Well, maybe he saw what you saw. That night . . . the red eyes or whatever?" I can tell that Ryan feels dumb even bringing this up as a serious answer, but I don't.

"Maybe," I say. "It could've been what killed that bear, too."

"No way," Ryan scoffs. "I think it's got to be just a really big cougar, or a pack of wolves or something."

"I know what I saw out there," I say. "It wasn't a

cara lockwood

wolf, and besides, that kid said 'monster.' Didn't you hear him?"

"Yeah, but I mean, come on, monsters don't exist."

I feel annoyance bubble up in me. Ryan is always so practical. He never thinks outside the box. I suppose this is what I should expect from Mr. Popular, and yet, I can't help but find it seriously irritating. Why doesn't he just believe me? Heathcliff would believe me, I think. He'd believe me, unconditionally. He wouldn't assume I was an idiot. Unlike Ryan, who is giving me a look like he thinks I belong in a remedial class.

"Don't you see that this place isn't normal?" I ask him, teetering very close to blurting out the school secret. "I mean, your basketball coach disappears. We're stuck on an island known for causing shipwrecks, *and* people think they see monsters? Don't you think that something isn't right here?"

"Miranda—come on." Ryan sighs, rolling his eyes. "You can't honestly believe that. It sounds like you've been listening to one too many campus legends. Next you're going to tell me that you see ghosts or something."

"Oh, forget it." I sigh, stabbing at my dinner in frustration. Ryan can be so thick-headed sometimes. I just want to shake him. Suddenly I feel a great space between us. I really, really wish Heathcliff were here. I wouldn't have to explain myself to Heathcliff.

"You're just letting your imagination run wild," Ryan says, giving my hand a little patronizing pat. I only just manage not to stab his hand with my fork. I wonder how calm he'd be if he faced down Dracula. I have a sudden desire to take him into the vault. I would love to see the look on his face when characters started popping out of books. Let's see how patronizing he'd be then. But I know I can't do that . . .

I sigh.

"Let's just talk about something else," I say.

Outside the cafeteria, we bump into Blade, Hana, and Samir. Hana sees me first, and starts with, "Hey, we've got news . . ." but then abruptly trails off when she sees Ryan.

"What news?" Ryan asks, looking between Hana, Samir, and me.

"Um, we, uh . . ." Hana starts, but then trails off, not sure she wants to finish in Ryan's presence. It must be LIT business.

"Some kid saw a monster," Blade says, not blinking. "We think it was your monster. The one you saw."

"Oh, not you guys, too." Ryan sighs again, exasperated. "Next you're going to say you got kidnapped by a UFO, or we're all already dead and don't know it. I mean, don't tell me you believe in Santa Claus, too."

Blade quirks an eyebrow and shoots me a look. I roll my eyes. I mean, what can I say? When it comes to the paranormal, my boyfriend is totally clueless.

"Um, *okay*," Blade says. "I think somebody needs a time-out."

"Ryan! *There* you are," Parker calls, walking up to my boyfriend and putting her arm through his. "You promised you'd walk me to the gym. With that maniac on the loose, and now who knows what—a cougar? I just don't feel safe."

Hana scoffs and Blade makes gagging noises, like she's going to vomit. Parker sends her a sharp look. Blade just wrinkles her nose at Parker, and sticks out her studded tongue.

"Miranda . . ." Ryan says, sending me a sheepish, apologetic look.

"Whatever! Go, I don't care," I say, waving my hand. I'm tired of fighting Parker for Ryan. And frankly, after dinner, I'm a little tired of Ryan, too.

When the two of them leave, Hana grabs my arm. "You're just going to *let* them go?" she asks me.

"I can't *make* him stay if he doesn't want to stay," I say. "Besides, I've had my fill of Ryan for the moment. For one thing, he doesn't believe in ghosts."

"He's in the wrong place then," Samir says.

"Forget him," Blade says. "Jocks never have any imagination. Besides, we have more news. We talked to at least five students, and they all agree on the last person to see Coach H. And it's a guy in a hooded sweatshirt. We think it's the stalker. He was talking to Coach H, apparently, before Coach H disappeared."

"What does the stalker want with Coach H?"

"Maybe Coach H had caught him, and was going to call the cops," Hana says.

"Maybe, or maybe he's someone else," I say, wondering if the stalker is Heathcliff; then he'd have a different motive altogether for silencing Coach H.

"Okay, you know something you're not telling us," Hana says. "I *know* you're keeping something from us. So spill it."

"Well . . ." I think it's about time I fessed up about my initial thought that Heathcliff might be the stalker, but I just can't seem to find the words.

"Wait, you know Hooded Sweatshirt Stalker!" Blade exclaims. "You know who he is and you haven't told us!"

"Yeah, well, at least I *thought* I did," I say. "I have a confession to make, and I think you guys had better sit down."

Fourteen

They take the news that Heathcliff is alive better than I thought.

"That maniac is on the loose and you didn't tell us!" Blade shouts, throwing down her backpack to show how angry she is. Samir looks like he might faint, and Hana just shakes her head in silent disapproval. Since Heathcliff kidnapped the three of them and bound and gagged them, he's not exactly among their top friends on MySpace.

"I didn't know how to tell you," I say.

"You mean you didn't *want* to tell us," Hana says, quietly. "You're still protecting him."

"I'm not . . ." I protest, but it's useless. Hana doesn't believe me.

"You realize he's psychotic," Blade says. This coming from my roommate with the pink hair and the lame Wiccan spells.

"He did save my life," I point out. "Multiple times."

"And he nearly killed all of us," Samir says. This is also true.

"Not to mention destroy the world as we know it," Hana points out.

"Yes, but he did end up saving everyone, and the world," I say.

Hana sighs. "You're still heavily under the influence of his bad-boy mojo," she says sadly and shakes her head.

Maybe she's right. Maybe I am.

"I thought you were over him," Hana continues, looking frustrated. "Does Ryan know about him?"

"No."

"Are you going to tell him?"

"I don't know."

"I just don't understand how he's still in this world," Samir says. "I thought *Wuthering Heights* was destroyed." Samir's talking about the vault version of the book, the one that allowed Heathcliff to come into this dimension in the first place.

"A small part of it must have survived," I say, not adding that the piece of a page from that book is in the locket I'm wearing around my neck. Given their reaction to the general news that Heathcliff is roaming the campus, it's probably not a good idea to tell them I'm in possession of the one piece of paper that could send him back to his own world.

"I can't believe you kept this from us," Hana says, shaking her head. "We've got to tell Ms. W."

"I don't think that's a good idea," I say.

"You're not objective on this subject," Samir says.

"I can't believe you didn't think to mention it," Hana says. "And now look what's happened. Heathcliff has probably kidnapped Coach H. Or worse, destroyed his book, and his soul along with it."

"I don't think he'd do that," I say.

"There you go defending him again!" Samir smacks his forehead as if he can't believe what he's hearing.

"I think we may have to vote you out of the LITs," Blade says.

"Since when is that an actual club?"

"Since I made T-shirts," Blade says, showing us all the navy blue Bard T-shirts she's gotten from the bookstore. In silver permanent marker she's written "LITs Society" on the sleeve.

"You don't expect us to actually wear these," I say.

"Well, not you, since you're on probation," Blade says. "But the rest of us, yes."

"Guys, listen, I was going to tell you . . ." I start, feeling hopeless. They're all furious at me. And, I suppose, for good reason.

The three of them just glare at me, disappointment in their eyes.

"Whatever," Hana says finally, turning away from me. "Come on, guys, let's go see Ms. W."

"Let me go with you," I say as Samir and Blade start to leave.

"I think you've done enough already," Hana says, giving me a sad look as she follows Samir and Blade, leaving me alone on the library steps.

It's true that I should've told them all about Heathcliff. But how? I knew how they all felt about him, and I knew they'd want to tell the faculty, and the faculty, well, they will just want to find a way to banish him. And I guess I just feel like everyone else has taken an unfairly harsh view of Heathcliff. He is the one who saved us all, and it's like they just won't see that. Granted, I'm not completely naïve. I know he has a bad side. But I also know he has a good side, too.

In the second half of *Wuthering Heights,* he spends the entire time avenging himself on everyone he thinks has ever done him wrong, and he does so in a vicious, merciless way. But his true love had just died, so he had cause—sort of.

So I understand why people distrust him. But I just see him in a different way. Maybe it is his bad-boy mojo, or the fact that I'm related to Catherine, his true love, but I don't know. I see something different in him.

A week passes and Hana, Blade, and Samir continue to freeze me out, no matter how often I try to apologize. I'm not sure how to make amends, and the three of them don't want to tell me, either.

I want to tell Ryan what's going on, but I can't without telling him the secrets of Bard, which I swore to the faculty I wouldn't do. Not to mention, Ryan would outright laugh at me if I told him the truth—that Heathcliff is a fictional character from 1847.

And even if I left out the supernatural parts, it's not like Ryan wants to hear about Heathcliff. He's been semijealous of Heathcliff since last semester. If I even bring up Heathcliff's name, Ryan will change the subject. So if I told him I'd been hiding the fact that Heathcliff is still hanging around Bard, I'm sure he'd have the same reaction as Hana, Blade, and Samir did. The same or worse.

"So are you going to tell me what happened between you and your friends?" Ryan asks me as he walks me back to my dorm after dinner in a rare Parker-free moment.

"What do you mean?"

"I mean, like why they don't talk to you anymore and avoid me?"

"We just had a fight."

"About what?"

"I don't feel like talking about it."

"Is it about Parker? Because I really am sorry, I just don't know what to do. I don't want to be responsible in case something does happen to her."

"Yeah, sure, whatever," I say, waving my hand like I don't care. And I'm surprised to find that I don't actually care as much as I should. It's annoying, yes, but I've got bigger problems on my plate right now. Like trying to figure out if Heathcliff is the Hooded Sweatshirt Stalker or not.

Ryan gives me a sidelong glance. "By the way, I talked to Derek, and he won't be bothering you anymore."

I glance at Ryan and feel a rush of warmth. He's so *good*. Attentive and sweet and *good*.

"What did you say to Derek?"

"Let's just say he got the message. I know he's a bit of a slime, but he's not going to go anywhere near you."

"Thanks, Ryan," I say, and I mean it.

"Don't mention it," he says, waving his hand. "Now, come on, what's going on with you and Hana?"

"Nothing. Just girl stuff."

"And you and Samir?"

"Just drop it, okay?"

Ryan lets out a frustrated sigh, putting his hands into his shaggy hair. "Okay, *whatever*."

"What do you mean, 'whatever'?"

"Nothing," Ryan says, shrugging.

"No, go on."

"It's just that you get all upset about me not talking about . . . the car accident, but you have secrets, too. I mean, I'm not dumb. I know there's something going on with you guys, and it's something you don't want to tell me. Why?"

"You just have to trust me," I say. Hypocrite? Party of One? Since when is it okay for Ryan to have secrets, but not me? If he's withholding information, then I can, too. It's only fair.

"Fine, well, then you'll just have to trust me, too, I guess," Ryan says.

We stop in front of my dorm and eye each other. Normally this is the time that he'd try to steal a kiss. But tonight, both of us are in a mood.

"Well, guess I'll see you tomorrow then," he says, not making eye contact with me. Then, before I can respond, he turns on his heel and starts walking back the other way, leaving me alone in front of my dorm door.

I wonder who else I'm going to manage to piss off this week. I seem to have a knack for it.

*   *   *

When I get back to my room, Blade is sleeping, as usual. That girl can sleep at all times of the day or night, even when she's mad at me. I notice that despite the fact that we're not currently on speaking terms, Blade has still managed to dip into my snack reserves. The stash of M&M's and Doritos in my closet are decidedly low. Candy and snacks are prohibited on campus, but I managed to sneak some in from home.

I take a packet of M&M's from my stash and then settle down at my desk to start studying. I've got two papers and a midterm exam coming up, and with all the Coach H drama, I haven't started working on any of them.

As I start reading *The Crucible* and munching on M&M's (green ones first!), I swear I hear a distant roar. I put down the candy and I listen again. Yep, that's no bear growl out in the woods. That's something else.

I have a sudden vision of those red eyes. Is it that . . . thing?

I jump up and head to the window. All I see is the pitch-black of the woods. Somewhere in the distance, a flash of lightning streaks across the sky, illuminating the trees, followed by a deep rumble of thunder.

And then, in the silence that follows, I hear the sound of tree branches cracking. My room is on the second floor, about twenty feet from the woods. I peer into the darkness, trying to make out what might be making those sounds. It could, I reason, be a bear. Not that monster thing. And then I shake myself. Since when is a bear *preferable*? It's still a freaking bear.

Lightning flashes again and I see a great shadowy figure near the edge of the woods. At first, I can't quite tell what it is, it's just a dark blob. Then it starts to move. It walks like a cat. A really big cat. Correction: a really, really, *really* big cat. A cougar? I think I heard something about cougars being in the woods. But are they that big? It's the size of a small Volkswagen Beetle.

It's hunched over something. What is it doing? Smelling something? Eating? It's hard to tell. A bolt of lightning flashes in the sky, making everything bright for a split second. Do I see stripes? But wait . . . it's got something it its jaws.

Oh God.

I think that's—is it someone's tennis shoe?

Fifteen

I bolt from the window and tumble on top of Blade.

"Wake *up*," I hiss at her. "There's something out there."

Sleepily, Blade comes to. "Wha . . .?" she murmurs, rubbing her eyes.

"Outside. There's, well, a cat. Or something bigger than that. A tiger, or a cougar, or I don't know."

"What are you *ranting* about?" Blade moans, falling back in her bed. I have to physically tug her out of bed and press her sleepy face up against the window. But by the time I do, the cat, or whatever it was, is gone.

"It was there, I swear." I say. "Just a second ago. It had somebody's shoe."

Blade moans. "Great, well, when the 'shoe monster' comes back, *don't* wake me, okay? And by the way, just for this, I am giving you *double* the silent treatment tomorrow."

"I'm sorry, but I *did* see something out there."

"Silent treatment!" Blade shouts at me, then throws the covers over her head and rolls over, putting her back to me.

The next morning, I go straight out before breakfast and check out the line of trees by our dorm. There are paw prints in the mud, big ones.

"See? I told you something was here," I say, basically to myself since Blade wouldn't follow me out here. In fact, she wouldn't even acknowledge my presence this morning. I think she's angrier about being cheated out of sleep than me keeping Heathcliff's appearance secret.

I look for the shoe, but I don't see it. I also don't see any blood, which I take as a good sign. Maybe whatever that thing was, it just got it from the trash. The shoe didn't necessarily have to be attached to an actual person when the animal took it. Near one of the prints, I find another torn piece of paper.

It looks like something from the same drawing. I dig around in my blazer pocket and pull out the other three pieces. They all look like they're from the same drawing—the ones I found outside the gym, on the campus commons, and then in Coach H's room. Only this third piece looks like a claw, from a paw, maybe. Okay, so now I know these drawings have to be connected somehow to Coach H's disappearance, the Hooded Sweatshirt Stalker, and to whatever I saw last night. This can't just be a coincidence.

I need some answers, and maybe Ms. W has them. I look for her at morning assembly, but I don't see her. Strange. I decide to look for her later, at our counseling session this afternoon.

Sitting in biology class, I'm still thinking about the tiger or lion or cougar, or whatever it was I saw last night, even as I fiddle with the pieces of the drawing I've found around campus. I put them on my lab table and try to rearrange them. One, I think, is definitely a cat's ear. Another is a paw—for sure.

My concentration is broken when I hear Parker's name called by Mr. S, which stands for Stevenson, as in Robert Louis. Apparently, God or Headmaster B thought it would be apt to have the author of *Dr. Jekyll and Mr. Hyde* teach biology. As luck would have it, today we're discussing the reproductive habits of frogs while dissecting one. I don't think I need to tell you how disgusting this is.

"Parker, I've asked you a question," Mr. S says.

It is one of the great injustices of my life at Bard that I have two classes with Parker, when I don't even share a single class with Hana, Ryan, or Samir. The scheduling gods hate me.

Parker slowly looks up. "What?" she barks, as if she's the CEO of a Fortune 500 company talking to a lowly assistant who has just interrupted a board meeting.

"I asked you if you would like to tell us if this is a girl frog or a boy frog," he repeats, as he points to a slide on the overhead projector.

Parker just glares at him. She does this because she doesn't know the answer to his question. She never knows the answer to any question that doesn't involve designer shoes. She gets out of them typically by making a joke, or, in most cases, just ignoring the teacher altogether. When pressed, she'll say, "I don't *know*," as if knowing the answer would be a waste of time.

Now, however, she has a gleam in her eye. That can't be good.

"I don't *know*," she says. "Why don't you ask *Miranda*. I hear that she's supposed to be an expert on the male anatomy."

This causes some snickers in the room. Great. My rumors still haven't died down, I see. They're as funny as ever—to everybody else.

Mr. S looks around, confused. Apparently he's the only person on campus who hasn't heard the rumors. I feel my face turn bright red.

"In case you haven't noticed, we're dealing with frogs here, Ms. Rodham," Mr. S tells her.

"I'm sure someone with Miranda's *experience* can probably tell us about the genitals of just about any mammal."

This causes more snickers.

"Frogs are amphibians, not mammals," I say, but I don't think anyone but Mr. S hears me. This is why Parker—a junior—shares two of my sophomore classes. Because she doesn't know that frogs aren't mammals.

"That's right, Miranda, they are," he says, still a little puzzled about the innuendo in the room. That's what happens when your teacher's a ghost from the nineteenth century. Modern teen sex humor is lost on him.

I glance backward in class and see that Parker and her clones are continuing the joke, and every so often the group at their lab table starts laughing.

"Everyone, it's time to start the frog dissection," Mr. S says, clapping his hands together.

My lab partner is a girl named V (which stands for Veronica). She's got blue hair and five nose rings. Like Blade, she's a Goth, but unlike Blade, she isn't obsessed with the occult. V is not exactly a communicator. I don't think I've actually heard her speak more than two words at a time.

"Want to get started?" I ask V, about our dead frog

that's lying belly-up in a metal tray on the lab table we share. V just glares at me.

"I'll take that as a 'yes,' " I say.

Behind us Parker's table starts giggling. I glance back and see that Parker and her clone lab partner have attracted a crowd.

"Hey, Miranda," calls one of Parker's clones, "why don't you come take a look at this?"

"How about I don't?" I say. The last thing I want to do is give Parker the satisfaction of seeing whatever juvenile thing she's doing back there. She's probably drawing pictures of me in compromising positions with half the basketball team.

"Ms. Rodham?" calls Mr. S from the front of the class. "Something you'd like to share with the rest of the class?"

Uh-oh. Mr. S has just given Parker what she wanted: a spotlight. While most sane people feel public humiliation, Parker doesn't. She likes being the center of attention, and she usually uses it to burn someone else.

"Mr. S," Parker says, "we were just exploring the frog's reproductive system, using a visual aid."

The crowd from the table parts, to show the dissection tray. They've put one frog facedown in the groin of the other frog. The facedown frog has a sign stick-pinned to its back that reads "Miranda."

The whole class starts laughing.

"That's enough, Ms. Rodham. That'll be a detention

for you," Mr. S says, looking like he's not quite sure what's happened, but knowing it's something bad. "The rest of you . . . back to work."

Parker gives me a little triumphant smile. She doesn't seem to mind the fact that her little prank earned her a detention. Apparently the gloating rights were worth it.

"Clever," I say to her, meaning the opposite.

If there is a big cat stalking students on this campus, is it too much to ask for it to eat Parker first?

I shrug off Parker's antics. I've got bigger problems. Like whatever it was that I saw with a shoe in its mouth last night. Maybe Ms. W has some answers.

I head to Ms. W's office, but when I get there, I find no Ms. W.

Instead, standing over her desk with his back to me, is the Hooded Sweatshirt Stalker. I stop in my tracks. He's picking up a book from the desk, which he slips into his pocket.

This is the closest I've been to him since the night I saw him in Coach H's room. I realize being alone in a room with the would-be campus rapist isn't the smartest thing, but I just can't shake the feeling that he isn't attacking people. At least not how they think. Besides, it might be Heathcliff.

"What are you doing?" I ask, causing the hooded

figure to turn slightly, but I see no nose or chin, or anything that might identify him. He moves away from the desk, and away from me, toward the bookcase.

"Wait! Where are you going?" I grab his arm and try to tug him around to see his face, but he gives me a shove, and I fall back a few steps. Now I get a really bad feeling. I'm pretty sure whoever this is, it *isn't* Heathcliff. He wouldn't shove me. I'm almost positive. He'd never hurt me. And now, I start to think how dumb I am—being alone in a room with a would-be attacker.

He turns from me and pulls a book from the shelf of Ms. W's bookcase. The entire bookshelf slides to one side, revealing a stone passageway on the other side. A hidden door! I wonder if Coach H's room has one, too.

I decide the only thing to do is call for help. I start to shout, for Guardians, for anyone, and that's when Hooded Sweatshirt Guy whirls at me. He grabs me by both arms and shoves me, hard, against Ms. W's desk. The corner of the desk hits my back.

"Ow!" I cry, just as Hooded Sweatshirt Guy lifts his head.

And I find myself staring at the impossible.

I look at where Hooded Sweatshirt Guy's face should be, but there *isn't one.*

The Hooded Sweatshirt Stalker doesn't have a head at all.

Sixteen

I'm staring at the empty hood of the sweatshirt. He has no face, no head, no anything.

A scream gets stuck in my throat, just as I hear a familiar voice at the door of Ms. W's office.

"Hey!" shouts Hana. "Let her go!"

Hooded Sweatshirt Guy nods his hood at me, then lets me go. In two quick steps, he bounds out through the open passageway. A second after he's gone, the bookcase slides shut, completely sealing the passageway.

"Weird," Hana breathes, her eyes wide. She glances down at me. "Are you okay?" she asks me, helping me pull myself up from the desk.

"He . . . He . . ." I choke, trying to get out the words.

"What? Was it Heathcliff? Is that who you saw?"

I'm still shaken, and my voice doesn't seem to be working.

"N-n-no," I say, shaking my head. "He's not Heath-cliff. He doesn't *have a face*."

"He what?"

"No head. No face. Nothing. Just the sweatshirt."

"I think you need to rewind," Hana says.

I recap the last five minutes, and Hana listens.

"I don't know for sure, but I am almost positive that whatever happened to Coach H has also just hap-pened to Ms. W," I say. "I think she's missing, too."

Hana nods. "I noticed she wasn't at morning assem-bly."

"And by the way, thanks," I say. "For saving me from the Headless Sweatshirt Stalker."

"You're welcome—I guess." Hana frowns a little. She's still a bit mad about me keeping secrets from her.

"Hana, listen, I am *sorry,* okay? I am really, really, really sorry. Like, sorrier than I've been for anything. And I've told you this over and over, but I'm going to keep saying it until you forgive me, okay?"

"I like the groveling. The groveling works," Hana says, a smile creeping slowly across her face. "Any-way, I forgive you."

I can't help it, I hug Hana.

"I'm really sorry—I am."

"I know," she says, "besides, I had to take you back sometime. I was getting tired of hanging out with

Samir twenty-four-seven. I mean, I've heard every one of his fart jokes now, a hundred times."

"That's torture!"

"Tell me about it. Anyway, maybe we should try to follow the stalker?"

I move closer to the bookcase and try pulling down several books. None of them opens the door.

"You sure that's how he opened it?" Hana asks me.

"I thought so, but it's not working now."

"Maybe you have to be missing a head to be granted entrance to the secret passageway."

"Maybe," I say, growing frustrated that I can't make the bookcase move. Eventually I give up. "So what do we do now? About Ms. W and Coach H?" I ask her.

"I hate to say this, but I think we need to call a meeting of the LITs."

We meet Blade and Samir on the grass commons in front of the boys' dorm. Just this week the snow has melted, and patches of brown and yellow grass are now visible in the sun.

"This better be good, because it's freezing out here," Samir says, shivering. Samir has low cold tolerance. Even though the sun is out, and the icicles from the trees are melting steadily, he still would rather be inside with hot cocoa.

"First order of business, Miranda is back in the LIT fold," Hana says.

"How can you decide that? We have to put it to a vote," Blade says.

"Can we just get on with it?" Samir cries, sounding cranky. "Did I mention I am freezing here? What is it—negative twenty out here?"

"Okay, fine, we'll skip the voting," Blade says. "It's good to have you back," she adds.

"Are we going to all kiss Miranda's butt, or are we going to get down to business?" Samir asks. When I give him a sharp look, he adds, "What? I just have a low cold tolerance. You *know* I love you—in a strictly sexual way."

"Go ahead," Hana says, looking at me.

I tell them what I know so far, everything about the Headless Sweatshirt Stalker, Ms. W's disappearance, and the thing that might be a cougar with stripes roaming around campus.

"Cougars don't come with stripes," Blade points out.

"I'm not sure if that's what I saw, but it looked like it," I say.

"We also found a secret passageway in Ms. W's room," Hana adds. "Headless Sweatshirt Guy made his escape through it."

"Secret passageway! I knew it," Blade says.

Hana stares at her.

"What? I mean, this place screams out for secret passageways," she adds.

"We couldn't figure out how to open it, though. And anyway, we have more clues," I add, showing them the scraps of paper. "I've found these in both Coach H and Ms. W's rooms. And basically wherever Headless Sweatshirt Guy turned up. They have to mean something."

"But what?" Blade asks.

"I don't know. Something. I think that's an ear," I say, pointing to the one with a triangle.

"Wait a second," Blade says. She rips a piece of notebook paper out of her spiral notebook and puts it on the grass in front of us. She places the pieces on top of the paper and then arranges them one way, and then another. With a black marker, she draws the missing lines.

"It's a tiger," I exclaim, suddenly seeing the picture come into focus. "So that *is* what I saw then. It's not a cougar at all. It's a tiger. I thought it could be, but I just thought it was too far-fetched."

"Are there lions and bears, too?" Samir jokes.

"You're sure it's a tiger?" Hana asks. "I mean, what's a tiger doing at Bard?"

"It's *Bard*. Do we need a good reason?" Blade asks.

"Good point."

"Maybe these are clues to who is messing with the faculty," I say.

"Why would someone deliberately leave clues? And besides, we already know who the culprit is, don't we? It's Heathcliff." Hana glares at me, as if daring me to contradict her.

"But he's not the Hooded Sweatshirt Stalker," I say.

"Correction—Headless Stalker. But maybe he is, after all," Hana says. "You know that he's not very powerful now that *Wuthering Heights* has been destroyed. Maybe he's fading away, like the invisible man."

"I just don't think it's him," I say, not bothering to volunteer the fact that I have a part of a page from that book in the locket around my neck. "I can't explain it more than that."

"I can in three words," Hana says. "Bad-boy mojo."

"Can we get back to the tiger? Hel-lo!" Blade says, tapping her piece of paper.

Hana sighs. "Fine. Well, assuming that *is* a tiger, there are a few of them in literature. There's the tiger Shere Khan in Kipling's *The Jungle Book*. There's also a tiger in *Winnie-the-Pooh*."

"Christopher Robin at Bard? Even in this place that sounds wacky," I say.

"Technically, the author of *Winnie-the-Pooh* is A. A. Milne," Hana says. "And this tiger doesn't look like the friendly, hyperactive Tigger, does it?"

"No, it definitely doesn't," I say. We only have a few pieces of it, but it looks like a tiger of the more fierce variety. "Who else? Is there a poem, maybe? Or some kind of adventure story . . ."

"Wait," Hana says, as if getting an idea. "There is a poem about a tiger. A famous one. Tyger with a Y. 'Tyger, Tyger burning bright . . .' But I can't remember the rest. But it's by Blake. Yeah, William Blake."

"The same crazy Blake we have for theology class?" I ask. "You don't think that's a little bit of a coincidence?"

"Well, he is the only poet I can think of who was also an illustrator," Hana says. "He could've drawn this. He illustrated his own books of poetry, as well as Dante's *Inferno*."

"He has to be involved."

"Maybe," Hana says. "Or maybe Heathcliff is trying to frame him."

"You know, I'm not even going to try to defend him. Will this prove to you that I'm overcoming the bad-boy mojo?"

"It's a start," Hana says. "Come on, let's find Blake."

Seventeen

We find Blake erasing the board in his classroom, talking to himself. Correction: talking to his imaginary friend, the angel Gabriele. When we show him the pieces of the drawing, he frowns.

"Why, yes, this is one of my drawings, but where did you find it? I threw it away some time ago, which is why it's in pieces."

Hana shoots me a knowing glance. This is her way of telling me that Heathcliff is framing Blake.

"Can you tell us what the tiger means?" Hana asks him.

"Well, Gabriele knows the answer to that one," Blake says, starring out into the middle of the classroom to the spot, I assume, where his hallucination is standing, or floating, or whatever angels do.

Samir, a puzzled look on his face, glances to the middle of the room and then back to Blake.

"You see, I wrote the poem to prove how powerful God is. You see, God created the lamb, but God also created the tiger. Imagine the power of someone who would create something as strong and fierce as a tiger. I think, by the very fact that tigers exist, there is proof of an all-powerful God."

"Do you know anything about Coach H and Ms. W?" Hana asks Blake.

"I'm afraid, as a faculty member, I cannot talk about faculty business," Blake says. "But Gabriele can help you."

Samir looks at the empty spot in the room. "Gabriele can help us?" He sounds skeptical.

"Gabriele can show you the way." Blake points to one of the student desks in the classroom. There's a book laying on top of it. Hana picks it up and shows it to me. It says *Bard Academy Faculty Handbook*.

"What's this?" I ask Blake.

"A little heavenly illumination," Blake says.

"Wow, this is weird," Hana says as she flips through the book's heavy parchment paper while we walk back to our respective dorms. "It's like a rules and regulations book for ghosts. Listen to this," Hana says as she begins to read from the book. " 'The living shall not know about the dead. Knowledge of life after death could cause irrevocable damage to the psyche of the living.' "

"I guess we're damaged goods then," Samir says.

"As if that weren't already obvious," I say.

"Are you going to hog that book the entire time, or actually let someone else see it?" Blade cries. She's completely put out that Hana has in her possession a book of the undead and isn't sharing.

"Wait, listen to this, guys," Hana says, ignoring Blade. "According to this, teachers aren't allowed to use their ghost powers in front of the living. *Not even to save their lives.*"

"I guess Coach H and Ms. W broke those rules pretty soundly," Samir says.

I nod. Last semester they pretty much let it all hang out when they were trying to corner Dracula. It's the main reason we found out who they really are.

"Maybe something else is going on here. Something that maybe doesn't have to do with Heathcliff," Hana muses out loud. "What if the faculty are punishing their own? This handbook lists a number of punishments for breaking the rules, including banishment."

"You think Coach H and Ms. W are being punished for helping us last semester? For showing us their powers in order to save us?"

"But why did they wait so long? Why now?" Blade asks. "It doesn't make sense."

"I don't know, but I do know that I don't think we're supposed to have this book," Hana says. "It's like a handbook for the dead."

"Which is *exactly* why I should be the one reading it," Blade says.

"Just wait a second—you'll get your turn," Hana barks. Hana reads a bit more as we walk along. "Wait, there's a whole section here about dealing with fictional characters. Apparently, it's not all that uncommon for them to get loose. You can also conjure them up, too."

"We could summon more of your family," Samir teases.

"Funny—as in *not*," I say. "What about the 'end of the world' stuff?"

Hana flips through a couple more pages. "I don't know about end of the world, but it does say something here about a 'delicate balance' between the dimensions."

The bell above the chapel tolls, signaling the end of the academic day and the start of extracurricular time. "Crap!" I exclaim, remembering my schedule. "I'm late for newspaper."

"Go, we'll meet up with you later," Hana says, her nose deep in the book.

Newspaper, one of my mandatory extracurricular activities, is housed in a tiny office at the back of the library, where we put together stories. While most of the campus is completely computerless, here, we actually have two old PCs that are used to lay out the newspaper. These computers, however, aren't hooked up to the Internet, so there won't be any undue distractions from our studies. MySpace is a forbidden thing here. Given that most of the faculty are more than 150 years old, it's no surprise that they're leery of computers. Imagine your grandma's techphobia times a thousand.

The editor of the newspaper is a guy named Chad Perkins. He's kind of a hard-core dork in an overtly greedy kind of way. At his old school, he'd been the ringleader of a scam to sell papers and old exams. Chad's very smart, but apparently not smart enough to get away with it. He claims the exams-for-cash scam was just about earning enough money to get him more SAT prep courses. He's obsessed with going to Wharton, the business school at Penn, where Donald Trump went. That's why I imagine one day he'll have a cheesy reality TV show and his own helicopter.

"You're late," Chad says to me when I walk through the door. Chad is a stickler for time. He's also about four inches shorter than I am, so he can't really intimidate me too much.

"I know, sorry—biology class."

"That's what that smell is," he says, waving his arm in front of his face.

"Funny," I say. I pick up the latest copy of the *Bard Weekly*, and see that Parker has grabbed the front-page headline again with her "campaign against the campus stalker" story. Also on the front page is a small story about sightings of a big cougar around campus. I read the story carefully, but there's nothing in it that I don't already know. And besides, I'm pretty sure now it's a tiger, not a cougar, that's on the loose.

"Do you fact-check these at all?" I ask him, holding up the paper.

"As little as possible," Chad says. "By the way, I've got some bad news for you, sweetheart."

"What is it?"

"Derek Mann's editorial column," he says, nodding toward the computer screen in front of him. He hits PRINT and sends the copy to the printer near his desk.

"Wait—Derek can write?" I joke. It's a well-known fact that most of the jocks at this school aren't known for their literary talents. All except Ryan, who happens to be a straight-A student.

"It's his guest column. He's written about you."

"He's WHAT?" I shout, snatching the paper from the printer.

"Don't say I didn't warn you," he says.

Chad is right. Derek has written a column about me. An *entire* column. And it's about . . . abstinence.

That's right. Derek Mann, Bard's most famous mlut,

has written a column about abstinence. He writes that most adolescents' problems can be found in their "straying" from "God's will."

Since when is Derek Mann religious?

He actually names me by name and calls me an "unfortunate sinner" and a "descendant of Mary Magdalene."

"Is this some sort of joke?"

"No joke. That's his submission. He says he's found God."

The article says he's going to "turn away from his sinful past" and embrace a new, "sinless" future, and he implores all other Bard students to do the same. In fact, he asks for everyone to start wearing abstinence bracelets, to show their commitment to no sex before marriage. The end of the article asks *me* to be the first to commit by wearing the bracelet. It's a yellow rubber bracelet with a red A on it for Abstinence.

I can't believe this. I mean, Ryan said he was going to talk to Derek, but I didn't think that involved becoming born-again.

"I'm sorry you're in it, but people are going to want to read this issue," Chad says. "Derek Mann embracing abstinence? This will be the *most*-read issue of the *Bard Weekly,* ever."

"Chad, you can't *seriously* run this article."

"Why not?"

"For one, it's libelous. Against *me*."

"Sweetheart, I know this looks bad for you, but it's an *opinion* column, and technically he doesn't say anything *bad* about you. He just asks you to join his abstinence pledge."

"But he *implies* that I'm as big a slut as he is. He's playing on the fact that everyone's heard the rumors. You've got to nix this story."

"I can only do that on one condition," Chad says. "You fess up to the rumors. Write a first-person column about what happened."

"But the rumors *aren't true*," I say, for the hundredth time. "I can't write a column about what I don't know. It would be the shortest column you've ever printed. It would only have two words: nothing happened."

"Do you have a bigger story for me?" he asks evenly.

"I saw our Hooded Sweatshirt Stalker," I say.

"Did you see his face?"

He's got me there.

"Er, not exactly."

"Well, then, I guess I've got no choice but to run with Derek's then."

Chad gives me his best Donald Trump sleaze smile.

Eighteen

"Just what did you tell Derek?" I ask Ryan, who's covered in sweat—as usual—and sitting on the gym floor stretching his leg. It's after yet another practice. Mr. S is filling in for Coach H temporarily. The gym is mostly empty except for me and Ryan. Derek has long since gone and it's nearly curfew time.

"I told him that maybe he ought to rethink his life choices," Ryan says. "And I told him to leave you alone."

"Did you know he's gone all crazy Puritan? He's written a column for the school newspaper asking everyone to take an abstinence pledge."

Ryan laughs, but then he sees the serious look on my face and stops. "Seriously?" he asks, looking surprised.

"Seriously. And the worst part is, he asks *me* to join

him. To put my past aside and become a better person. He wants me to wear an abstinence bracelet."

"And do you want to wear it?"

"That's not the point."

"But what do you think about sex before marriage?"

"I think given that the median marrying age in this country is twenty-six, I'll probably have sex before I get married, yes. But I'm not sure I want to have it at fifteen, either."

"So you haven't . . ." Ryan starts, then stops. "So you . . ."

I realize we haven't had this conversation yet. The one where I admit to him that I'm a virgin. And this is so not how I imagined this conversation would go.

". . . so you're a virgin," Ryan finishes.

"Is that a problem?" I ask, starting to think it might be. Ryan looks thoughtful.

"No, it's not a problem," he says. I notice he doesn't say, "I'm a virgin, too," because he most definitely isn't. Someone like Ryan probably lost his virginity at twelve. "It just explains some things," he adds.

"Explains what?" Is being a virgin somehow like being defective?

"Nothing," Ryan says, but I know he's thinking something he isn't saying.

"So would you talk to Derek? Ask him to take me out of his column?"

"I just don't quite see the problem. First, you were upset that everyone thought you slept around, and now Derek is giving you an opportunity to be a big abstinence advocate so that everyone thinks you *don't* sleep around. I mean just what is the problem here?"

"What's the problem?" I can't believe what I'm hearing. Has Ryan lost his mind? Isn't it obvious? "It's just another way to cement the rumor that I'm a big raging whore."

"Look, Miranda. I think you're overreacting here."

"I can't believe you're taking Derek's side."

"I'm not taking anyone's side. I just think that maybe you're a bit oversensitive about sex." There's that slightly patronizing tone again, like the one he used when he tried to convince me there is no such thing as the bogeyman. "It's just not that big of a deal, and I think maybe you are making a big deal out of it because you haven't had it yet."

I cannot believe what I have just heard. Has Ryan just done the equivalent of telling me I ought to go sit at the kid's table, while the grown-ups talk? Can he be so out of touch not to understand how important and fragile a girl's reputation is?

"Is that what you think?"

"It's really no big deal, Miranda, it isn't," Ryan says. He takes my hand. "I think you're making a big deal out of these rumors because you're afraid I'm going to ask you to go to that next step. But I want you to know that we can go at whatever pace you're comfortable with."

On some level, I realize this is his idea of being nice. Understanding. But frankly, I've had enough.

"You know what *I* think?" I say. "I think you don't have to talk to me like I'm a baby. And you know what else I think? I think you *like* these rumors. That they make you feel big or something. And I think that you don't really want them to stop, because you like being the guy who can make girls do anything."

"How can you say something like that," Ryan sputters, turning red. "What on earth makes you think I *like* that my girlfriend is supposed to be a whore when I'm not even *getting any*?"

The instant it's out of his mouth, Ryan realizes the mistake he's made.

For a few seconds, we just stare at each other in stunned silence. Then I shrug out of his jacket and toss it at his feet, just as the tears start to well up in my eyes.

"Wait, Miranda . . ." Ryan calls, but I'm already gone, the gym doors slamming shut behind me.

Outside, I run straight into two beefy Guardians.

"You need to come with us," they say.

"But I didn't even do anything," I say, wiping a few stray tears from my face. "It's not even curfew yet."

"Headmaster B wants to see you," the other says, grabbing me by the arm.

My night, it seems, just went from bad to worse.

Nineteen

I have no idea what Headmaster B wants with me, but I guess I'm going to find out. In Headmaster B's office, it's not just the Headmaster who's waiting for me. Beside her is Mr. Thompson, the school bus driver and driver's ed teacher. Thompson (as in Hunter S.) wears orange aviator sunglasses and a green visor. He's a bit gangly and strange, but his voice sounds like he's smoked more cigarettes than my grandma Colleen. And next to him is Blake.

Uh-oh. Maybe he's finally told on us for sneaking around Coach H's room. I glance at him, but I can't read his face.

"I'm glad you called me, actually, because you really ought to know that there's a . . ."

"Tiger? Yes, we know."

"You *know*? There's a man-eating tiger roaming the woods and *you knew*?"

"Yes, and you can explain to us how you released him now. Mr. Blake is very worried."

I glance over at Blake, who doesn't make eye contact with me.

"Me? I didn't release any tiger. You should be asking the Headless Sweatshirt Stalker. He's the one who has all the drawings."

"Headless who?" Blake asks.

"They guy in the sweatshirt. The guy who's supposedly attacking Bard students? The guy who doesn't have a face? You haven't heard of him?"

"Of course we have," Headmaster B says, dismissively. "But you and I both know it's Heathcliff and he's causing mischief. We warned you how dangerous he could be if left in this world."

"He's *not* the stalker," I say, but even I sound a little unsure.

"It's convenient, don't you think, that his first victim was Parker Rodham, your known rival?"

"But it's *not* him. I saw him and—"

"So you *have* spoken with Heathcliff," Headmaster B says, as if I've just fallen nicely into the trap she laid.

"No, that's not what I'm saying. I mean that—"

"We know you did it," Thompson interrupts in his

gravelly voice. "Tell us what you did with them."

"With who?"

"You know who," Thompson says. "Hemingway and Woolf. Where are they?"

"But I didn't—"

"We know that you had reasons to dispatch them both," Headmaster B says. "She told you of our suspicions of you, and you had to get rid of her so that she wouldn't tell us just how involved you were in this plot."

"But that's not true," I say. "I mean, it's true she told me that you suspected me, but I would never do anything to hurt her."

"I told you she'd be trouble," Thompson says. He doesn't like me, I can tell. "We can't just have students running around knowing about the vault. *Especially* fictionistas."

"Fictionistas?" I echo.

"Descendants of fictional characters," Headmaster B explains.

"There's more than just me?" I ask, perplexed. Is this true? Are there other people walking around with fiction-turned-real ancestors? And here I thought I was all alone. Then again, if the *Bard Academy Faculty Handbook* is right, then fictional characters aren't so strange to this world.

Headmaster B waves her hand as if dismissing the

entire subject. She clearly doesn't want to elaborate. "Miranda, these are serious charges leveled against you. We're going to have to have a faculty hearing."

I must look puzzled, because Thompson adds, "It's the most serious judicial proceeding at Bard Academy. You could get expelled."

At first, this sounds like my ticket out of here. Expulsion doesn't seem like such a bad thing. But then I remember Dad giving me a lecture over Christmas break. During one of the only visits where I saw him, he told me that if I don't make this work, then he's pressing charges for me wrecking his car, and I could go to juvie jail. I'm pretty sure it's the only place on earth worse than here.

"But I'm innocent," I say.

"If you are, then you have nothing to fear from a hearing," Headmaster B says.

I'm not so sure about that. It feels like there are forces at work here that are out of my control.

"Miss Tate, the hearing will be held in two days," Headmaster B says. "I suggest you rally a defense."

Twenty

"This is bad," Blade says in our room later. Hana is also there, flipping through the faculty handbook.

"It's worse than bad," Hana says, tapping her finger on an open page. "This says that you face 'figurative expulsion.' "

"The dead-to-us punishment? Ouch," Blade says, rolling over on her bed. "You know that's all BS. They 'expel' you, but they still get to keep your tuition money. It's such a scam!"

"Says here that you can call witnesses on your behalf," Hana continues, reading more from the handbook. "Maybe we could call Ryan."

"Um, yeah, I don't think he'd be up for it," I say.

"Why not?" Blade asks.

"We kind of broke up," I say.

"You *what*," Blade and Hana both say in unison.

"We had a fight. About the sex rumors. He was kind of a jerk about it."

"Ryan? A jerk? Are you sure we're taking about the same guy?" Hana asks.

Blade elbows her. "All guys can be jerks," Blade says. "It's embedded in their Y chromosome."

"I still can't believe you broke up with him," Hana says, shaking her head.

"Um, aren't you supposed to automatically take my side?" I say.

"I'm sorry. I'm just stunned. I mean, it's Ryan Kent we're talking about."

"I know. I know." I sigh. "It's complicated."

"This better not have anything to do with Heathcliff," Hana says, giving me a sharp look.

"How can it? I haven't even seen him."

"Correction—you haven't seen his face because he doesn't have one," Hana says. "But that doesn't mean he couldn't still be the stalker. Maybe he's just a ghost now, but one that's still powerful enough to cast his bad-boy mojo spell on you."

"He hasn't, okay?" I say. I'm not even sure if Heathcliff is still alive at this point. And no matter how much I try to explain, I just know the Headless Sweatshirt Stalker isn't him. "Anyway, can we get back to my trial?"

"You're allowed the counsel of your faculty advisor," Blade says, reading from the open page of the faculty handbook on Hana's lap.

"But that was Ms. W, and she's missing," I say.

"You can also have one fellow student defender," Hana says.

"That should be Hana. She's the smart one," Blade says. "By the way, why don't you guys wear your LIT shirts for court?"

Hana and I just stare at Blade. "What? I'm just asking. I think they're cool."

My hearing takes place in the library, which is closed off to all students Friday afternoon. The panel judging me is led by Headmaster B, Blake, and Thompson. Their stone-faced expressions say they aren't going to be very sympathetic to my case.

"You sure you know what you're doing?" I ask Hana as she shuffles through her notes.

Hana pushes her black-framed glasses up on her nose. "No, but I don't see that anyone else is jumping up here to defend you."

"That fills me with confidence," I say.

"Just relax," Hana says. "You're innocent, so they can't really have any proof, now can they?"

This makes me feel a tiny bit better.

Headmaster B bangs a gavel against the table

where the faculty are sitting, signaling that the hearing has come to order.

"Miranda Earnshaw Tate, you are charged with involvement in the disappearance of Virginia Woolf and Ernest Hemingway," Headmaster B begins, with no preamble. "The evidence against you includes the fact that you had a disagreement with Coach H the day before his disappearance over a grade you felt you didn't deserve. Is this true?"

"Yes, but I was framed, it wasn't—"

"Please, just answer the question yes or no," Headmaster B admonishes.

"Yes," I say reluctantly.

"And is it true that Ms. W discovered your involvement with Coach H's disappearance and confronted you the very week she disappeared?"

"No, that's not what—"

"You deny that Ms. Woolf confronted you?"

"She thought I was innocent. She was only trying to warn me."

"She was trying to warn you?" asks Thompson, who has skepticism written on his face. "Don't you think it's more likely that she wanted to prove to herself that you were the culprit, and to gather evidence for us?"

I look at each of the faculty members' stoic faces. I glance over at Hana. She stands up.

"Permission to speak," she says to the panel.

"Granted," Headmaster B says, waving her small hand.

"I have been good friends with Miranda since she came to Bard last year, and I know much of her relationship with Ms. Woolf. In fact, Ms. Woolf talked to me about Miranda three weeks ago."

I glance over at Hana. She never told me that.

"Before her disappearance, Ms. Woolf confided in me that she was worried about Miranda."

"Because of her suspicions that Miranda was plotting against the faculty?" Mr. B asks.

"No, because she thought Miranda was being framed," Hana says.

Other teachers in the library murmur and whisper to one another. Headmaster B frowns.

"And just who did she believe was trying to frame Miranda?" Headmaster B asks.

"I don't know, but we think it has something to do with the tiger . . ." Hana starts, but before she can finish, she's cut off by Headmaster B.

"You mean the tiger that Miranda conjured by using Blake's drawings? The pieces you showed to Blake himself?"

"Yes, but I *found* them. I didn't steal them," I say.

Blake speaks. "I for one agree with Ms. W. I think someone *is* trying to frame Miranda," he says. This causes more whispers in the audience. "Gabriele, who is God's right-hand messenger, who sees everything, has told me so."

For once, something for *my* side. But why is Blake defending me?

"And, honestly, we really don't have any reason to seriously suspect Miranda of lying," he says. "She's been nothing but truthful with us in the past."

Hana gives me a quick glance. I've been *mostly* truthful is what that glance tells me. I can't help but feel a pang of guilt here. I did keep the news of Heathcliff a secret. I look down and see that I'm nervously fiddling with the locket he gave me. I drop it and put my hands in my lap.

"We know she has fiction in her blood, but this doesn't mean that she isn't trustworthy on her own merits . . ." Mr. B fades off in the middle of his speech and his attention is drawn to the middle of the room, about six feet in the air, glancing up, as if someone is floating there. "Gabriele?" Blake asks the empty air. "What is it?"

Blake turns to look at me, as if the invisible angel has told him something.

"You say that she *has* misled us?" he asks the empty air. "But how?"

The faculty, including Headmaster B, all watch with curious faces.

"Objection!" shouts Hana suddenly. "Relevance of imaginary friend in hearing?"

"There are no objections in faculty hearings, Ms. Mura," Headmaster B chides. "And ghostly apparitions are admissible in faculty panel hearings, whether visible or not."

"But imaginary and-or not-seen figures are not allowed to testify in front of a faculty hearing," Hana argues, pushing her point. "It's in the handbook."

There are a few gasps among the faculty. "*Where* did you get that, Ms. Mura?" thunders Headmaster B. "Students are not allowed to see that!"

Guardians step forward and take the book from Hana's hands.

"But, Mr. Blake—"

"May I continue now?" Blake says, cutting off Hana before she can finish her sentence.

"We will deal with your infraction later," Headmaster B tells Hana. "In the meantime, continue, Mr. Blake."

He turns his head to the side, as if his imaginary angel friend is whispering into his ear. Blake nods, lets out a low whistle, and then nods again. He clears his throat. "Thank you, Headmaster. Now, Gabriele tells me that you've been keeping a secret from us. A secret that is contained in that locket you wear around your neck."

I swallow, hard. He may have me there. Hana glances over at me, with a puzzled look on her face. Now I really wish I had told her about the locket when I told her about Heathcliff. I know she's not going to take this news well. Not at all.

"Hand over the locket for inspection, Ms. Tate," Headmaster B commands.

Instinctively I wrap my hands around the locket protectively. "No," I say. "It's mine."

"Give it here," she adds, a bit more forcefully. And, even as I'm holding the locket, I feel the chain unclasp itself from my neck and fly, out of my hands on its own power, toward Headmaster B's outstretched hand.

"Hey, you can't do that!" I say, even though it's clear she just has.

Headmaster B inspects the locket and opens it. She looks at its contents and then at me.

"Heathcliff!" she says, and the faculty gasp. Headmaster B holds up the corner of the page of *Wuthering Heights* with his name printed on it, and shows it to the faculty in attendance. There are more whispers and murmurs. Next to me, Hana goes white.

"Ms. Tate, would you explain to us how you came to wear the only remaining piece of *Wuthering Heights*?"

"Miranda, you didn't . . ." Hana says, sounding sad. She slumps in the chair next to mine and puts her head in her hands.

"Would you care to explain why you did not tell us of Heathcliff's return? Or that you had the power to send him back?"

"I . . . uh . . . I think it's the bad-boy mojo," I say, because I can't think of anything else.

"Bad-boy what?" Headmaster B asks, perplexed.

"Never mind." I sigh. I doubt I can explain bad-boy mojo to Charlotte Brontë. "I have no justifiable explanation."

"Very well," Headmaster B says. "Based on this overwhelming evidence of deceit, I'm afraid the faculty board has no choice but to punish you, until such time as you agree to tell us what you or Heathcliff have done with the faculty members who are missing. Faculty, I ask for a vote. All in favor of figurative expulsion, raise your hands."

As I watch with dread, most of the faculty in the room raise their hands.

"Miranda Earnshaw Tate," Headmaster B continues, "I hearby sentence you to a semester of figurative expulsion. You shall not talk to or interact with any other students until deemed acceptable by the faculty. Your whereabouts will be monitored at all times. This punishment will be in effect until you decide to tell us what has happened to our fellow faculty members."

"But I don't know what happened to them—" I cry.

"Silence! You are no longer allowed to address any-one on this campus. From here on, you are invisible."

Guardians rush at me then, and one of them roughly tugs a red sweater vest over my head.

Headmaster B slams down her gavel on the table, signaling the end of the hearing and my life as I know it.

Twenty-one

Figurative expulsion is even worse than I thought. Hana isn't even allowed to talk to me when I leave the library. Even as I shout that I'm sorry about the necklace, that I had been meaning to tell her, she's held by a Guardian, so she can't even look me in the face. I don't know if she's mad or not.

My red V-neck sweater vest that I now have to wear officially makes me the campus pariah. While I generally love not wearing what everyone else is wearing, this is different. I stand out like a red M&M in a sea of blue ones. And people part in front of me, like I've got a contagious disease. No one wants to make the mistake of even appearing to talk to me, and face the same punishment.

In the course of a month, I've gone from being the

person that everybody stares at to the person everyone ignores.

I have to move out of my room with Blade, and into a single, barely big enough for a bed and a desk, all to myself. Since I can't talk to people, I'm prohibited from playing sports or other school activities, so all I do is eat, sleep, and study. Normally I'm the queen of all couch potatoes, but getting barred from everything but sleeping and studying pretty much blows. Time ticks by at a glacial pace.

Every day at morning assembly, Headmaster B reminds everyone at Bard not to talk or look at me, and that's basically the only time during the day my name is ever called.

I eat, sleep, and study completely alone, and it feels like the worst kind of solitary confinement. My only company is the new edition of the *Bard Weekly,* which just so happens to have Derek's column in it.

The headline reads: "Miranda: Change Your Sinning Ways."

While I'm eating at my own empty table in the cafeteria, I crumple up the paper, just in time to see a couple of juniors at a nearby table snicker. They're reading the article and looking over at me.

This stinks.

I can't even defend myself.

The no-talking rule extends even to teachers. I don't get called on in class. And if I have a question and raise my hand, the teacher just ignores me, like I'm invisible. It makes asking for bathroom breaks during class pretty much impossible.

I have to find a way to squeeze them in between classes, which means I have to take the quickest pit stops on record, since my classes are placed at opposite ends of the campus. It's like a drunk person made up my schedule.

On one of my hasty breaks in the girls' room I discover I'm the subject of graffiti I find on the wall.

> Ryan Kent plays ball,
> His girlfriend has the gall,
> To get to wear his jacket,
> She let the whole team dunk in her basket,
> And now she's all alone
> So she must atone.

"Dunk in her basket"? That's the best they could do? That has to be the worst poem ever, even by bathroom graffiti standards.

Ugh. Can my life get any worse?

In the mailroom, I find no letters from my friends or mom or even sister. I can't expect them to write me every day (I just got two letters the day before yesterday), but still, I can't help but feel a pang when I see a mostly empty mailbox. There's only one letter in it. When I pull out the envelope, I'm immediately disappointed to see the return address is my dad's office.

I should be glad that he's finally written me, but I know it can't be anything but bad news.

I open the letter. It says:

Miranda:

I'm glad you are making progress at Bard. However, neither Carmen nor I believe you are yet responsible enough to have the privilege of learning how to drive.

I don't think I need to remind you that I'm still dealing with the repercussions of you stealing and wrecking my BMW. Not to mention taking Carmen's credit cards without permission. You violated our trust. If your grades continue to improve this semester, we'll see if it's possible to revisit driving lessons at a later date.

Sincerely,
Dad

That's my dad for you. He can't even write "Love, Dad" because that would be showing too much emotion. I crumple the letter in my hand. My dad doesn't write me at all for months and this is the first letter he gets around to bothering to write? One talking about how immature I am? He has no idea the kind of responsibilities I've had since coming to Bard. Um, hello—fighting Dracula and managing to save the universe? I think I can handle a stick shift, thanks.

And Carmen! Since when does Wife Number Three's opinion matter? She's barely older than I am, and the only decisions she's well-informed enough to make involve shoe shopping.

Sometimes I seriously hate my dad. I know I shouldn't care what he thinks. I mean, since he ran off with his secretary five years ago, abandoning me, my mom, and my sister, he pretty much gave up all of his credibility as a parent figure.

I try to be Zen about it, but there's something about Dad that always manages to get under my skin.

I find at night that I can't sleep well, either. After I toss and turn for what seems like hours, I fall into a fitful sleep where I dream of the horseshoe-shaped tree again, and hear Heathcliff shouting for help. I wake up to the sound of the bell tolling. It's Sunday, and that means a late breakfast.

Once inside the cafeteria, I see that Parker has taken a seat right next to Ryan, which I could've predicted. What else would she do? I'm out of the picture.

I glance down at my red sweater vest and wonder what would happen if I just ripped it off and tore it to pieces.

After a lonely meal of questionable taste (something that looks like gruel), I don't feel like going back to my dorm to study. I've never so badly wished for a TV. I need to take my mind off of things. If I were at home, I'd head to the mall for some retail therapy, but since I can't do that, I have to settle for a slow walk on campus. Since I'm in no hurry to get back to my dorm, I notice a sign I hadn't seen before. Near the woods, it's a small wooden sign that says TO THE RIVER—CREW TEAM AND SUPPORTERS ONLY and an arrow pointing down a dirt trail that leads back into the forest.

It dawns on me that my recurring Heathcliff dream takes place near the river. I wonder, if I got a closer look would it help me make sense of my dream? I give a backward glance to the two Guardians who are following me at a distance, and decide to walk on ahead and see if they stop me.

They don't.

I pass the sign and head down the trail, and they follow at a bit of a distance. I expect one of them to shout, or tackle me, but neither does. I thought the forest was off-limits, but apparently this trail is okay. Neither of the Guardians seems too worried that I'm going to run away.

Not that escape is really plausible. We are, after all, on Shipwreck Island, at least five miles away from the Maine shore. Even if I jumped in the river and took it all the way out to the sea, I'd die of hypothermia before I made it to shore. The Atlantic is freezing and the currents are too strong.

The trail is dark and the trees around and above me are thick and tall, blocking out nearly all sunlight. Something is wrong with the forest, and it's not just because the trees seem unnaturally thick and tall. It takes me a while to realize that I don't hear any typical forest sounds. There aren't any birds chirping or frogs croaking. All around me is a distinctly eerie silence. The only sounds I hear are my feet on the gravel trail. I get the distinct impression I'm being watched, and not just by the Guardians behind me.

I remember the first night I spent at Bard Academy. I marched straight into these very woods, thinking I'd escape. I found out then they weren't like normal woods. Then again, what would I expect from a forest in purgatory?

I walk a little farther and I hear the sound of the river, a soft, bubbling water sound. The river comes into view and it's dark and wide; the water seems nearly black. There's a boathouse on the shore, where I assume the crew team keeps their gear. I pick up a smooth rock from the ground and try to skip it across the river, but as soon as it touches the water, it sinks. I throw another one. This one skips once, and then an enormous black fish leaps up from the surface of the water and swallows the stone—whole.

I take a surprised step back.

What the hell was that?

Before I can figure it out, I hear a faint shouting. It sounds like someone calling for help. In fact, the voice sounds a lot like Heathcliff.

I stop and turn.

The Guardians are standing several paces behind me. They don't seem to have heard the shouts. Maybe I imagined it.

I crouch down, pretending to look for skipping rocks, and I listen. There. That's definitely Heathcliff. And he's in trouble.

I try to zero in on Heathcliff's voice, but I can't figure out where it's coming from. Just when I think I'm sure it's coming from the river, then it sounds like it's off in the woods.

The Guardians keep their distance as I move away from the shore. When one of them turns to the sound of a tree branch cracking, I take the opportunity and make a run for it.

I dive straight into the heavy brush of the forest, zigzagging back and forth through the trees. Behind me, I hear the clamber of Guardians' footsteps, and their grunts and shouts as they try to follow me. I dive into a hollow tree and wait there, my chest feeling like it's going to explode from the sudden sprint. I wait there until my heart returns to normal, and I can't hear the sounds of the Guardians any more. When I'm sure the coast is clear, I backtrack, toward the river, and the boathouse.

And then, suddenly, I stop.

I find myself staring at a big boulder and the horseshoe-shaped tree. The very same boulder and tree that I've been dreaming about for weeks.

I glance around, looking for the church that's also in my dream, but it's not here. Instead, I see what looks like an old foundation, a series of brick stones set into a large square. This is where the church must have been.

The hairs on my forearms stand up and I get goose bumps on my arms.

Maybe my dream was *real*. Maybe I had been dreaming of this place. And maybe Heathcliff really is in trouble. I turn my attention to the boathouse, which isn't the church from my dream, but it's the only building standing here.

I walk around the boathouse, looking for a way in. I find one and step into the dusty boathouse, my mouth suddenly dry.

"Heathcliff?" I whisper before I can stop myself.

The boathouse is so quiet, my whisper sounds like a shout.

Inside there are white crew boats hanging upside down on top of one another on ledges. It's quite a big storage house, even bigger on the inside than it looks from the outside. Sunlight slashes through the dust on the floor in front of me, and I get the sudden, distinct impression that I'm not alone.

"Heathcliff? Are you in here?" I whisper again, this time a little louder. My heart is beating faster in my chest. I don't know why. I shouldn't be afraid of Heathcliff. He saved me more times than I can count. Still, I think about the faceless Hooded Sweatshirt Stalker and shiver.

"Hello? Anyone here?" I say again, this time louder. I hear what sounds like a muffled groan from above my head somewhere. I look up, but all I see are rafters. I take a few more steps and see a staircase, leading up to a loftlike office. I hear a clatter coming from the office. Someone is definitely in there.

As I head to the stairs, I hear a clatter behind me. Something has knocked into the row of boats hanging on the wall.

Something big.

I whip my head around and see a black-and-orange flash between the crew boats. I freeze. The tiger!

And then I hear Heathcliff's voice again, muted this time, but distinct, coming from the top of the stairs.

I pause on the staircase landing, my hand on the rail. Can I make it to the top of the stairs before the tiger sees me? I wish my sister Lindsay were here. She watches every Animal Planet special known to man. She'd know about the land speed of a tiger.

I close my eyes and burst ahead, taking the stairs two at a time, hoping that the office at the top of the staircase is open.

At the top of the stairs, I swing open the office door and then shut it hard behind me, slamming my whole weight against it. Then it occurs to me that if there *is* a tiger out there somewhere, and he wants in to this office, I'm probably not going to be able to just hold the door closed. Slowly I scoot up, and glance out through the door's window. There's nothing on the landing, or on the stairs. The tiger didn't follow me.

I let out a small sigh of relief and glance around the office, looking for something to shore up the door with.

That's when I see a crew boat sawed in half, laying facedown on the floor, and it seems to be groaning. I turn the boat over. Beneath it, I see a guy, tied up, with his back to me.

Gently, I roll him over.

He's got dust in his hair and a gag in his mouth, but I'd recognize those dark curls and those fierce black eyes anywhere.

It's Heathcliff.

166   cara lockwood

Twenty-two

"Heathcliff!" I cry, frantic. He looks dazed and out of it. I wonder how long it's been since he's eaten anything. And by his bruised face, it looks like someone has been manhandling him. I desperately try to free his hands and legs, but the ropes are too thick. I head to the nearby desk, where I search for anything sharp. I come up with a pair of scissors, but even then it takes me a while to cut through the thickly layered ropes.

Once I get his gag free, and his arms, Heathcliff just slumps to the side.

"Heathcliff! Can you hear me? Are you okay?" I ask him, helping him into a sitting position. His eyes flicker and he groans again.

"Catherine?" he chokes out.

"No, it's Miranda. Remember? *Miranda*," I say as

his eyes flicker open, wider this time. Recognition flitters through them as he looks into my eyes and then strokes my cheek with one finger. He gives me a weak smile.

"Miranda," he says and sighs, coming to a little more. "I knew you'd find me," he adds, and then passes out.

"Heathcliff!" I call, shaking him a little, but he doesn't come through. I've got a bottle of water in my backpack (courtesy of the Bard cafeteria) and I grab it and put a little on the sleeve of the sweatshirt, which I use to pat his forehead, and try to get him to come to. He groans again and his eyes flicker.

"Can you drink? You need to drink," I tell him, holding the water bottle up to his dry lips. He raises his head a little and takes a sip. After a few seconds, he takes a deeper swig. He seems to be coming around.

"Who did this? Was it Coach H?"

Heathcliff shakes his head from side to side.

"Ms. W? Headmaster B?"

"No." Heathcliff chokes, sitting up a bit. He downs the rest of the water bottle. "It wasn't them. They would've finished me. It was someone else."

"You don't know who?"

"I was in the woods. And I got jumped by a . . ." Heathcliff shakes his head as if he still can't quite believe it. "A tiger."

"A tiger? Attacked you?" I think about what I saw down below. The tiger might just be guarding Heath-cliff.

"Knocked me unconscious," he says. "When I woke up, I was here, tied up. That was two months ago."

"Did anyone feed you?" I ask, beginning to wonder if he'd been here all this time without food and water. But that's impossible, isn't it? Even for Heathcliff.

"A man came, to give me water and some food, but I don't know him," Heathcliff says. "He hasn't been here in a while."

"Did you see him? Do you know what he looks like?"

Heathcliff shakes his head. "He came alone, but he would talk to someone he called Gabriele."

"Blake!" I exclaim. "So Blake *is* behind this."

"Who's Blake?"

"A crazy faculty member—it's a long story," I say.

"He left those," Heathcliff says, nodding over in the direction of the desk in the corner. I walk over and find it's stuffed with drawings of tigers—all kinds. They match exactly the color and style of the pieces of paper I've been finding around campus. And even more unsettling, they're all signed by Blake.

It dawns on me that Blake has got to be involved in this whole thing. It's *his* tiger, and he's also the one who railroaded me at my hearing. I know I'm not the one animating the tiger. Chances are, either he's behind this or he knows who is.

I turn back to Heathcliff.

"Can you stand? Are you strong enough? We should get out of here."

As I help Heathcliff to his unsteady feet, I hear a growling sound on the other side of the office door. Heathcliff's head snaps up. He puts his finger to his lips to show me to be quiet and then he puts himself between me and the door.

He's half-dead and he's still trying to protect me.

I hold my breath, as I listen to what sound like paw-steps outside the door. Along the windows in front of the desk, I see black-and-orange ears go past, as well as his long, thick tail. That is *definitely* a tiger.

The tail stops and flicks back and forth. It's like he's trying to listen for us. Like he can hear us breathing.

Without making a sound, Heathcliff takes the water bottle that he's half finished, screws the cap on, and then hurls it through the open window to my left. It hits the tree outside with a thud. The tiger's head bounces up, ears perked. And then, in a flash, it leaps through an open window and jumps out to the tree limb less than a foot from the boathouse. It makes the jump with ease. The tree branch shudders under its weight, but the leaves of the tree almost entirely hide it. All I see is a tail, flicking back and forth, from beneath the tree limb.

In a rush, Heathcliff picks himself up and closes the window shut, latching it, but the tiger seems completely unperturbed. Either he doesn't care about us, or he's much happier in his tree.

"Now what?" I ask Heathcliff, who once again has his trademark scowl on his face. I think he's feeling better, at least better enough to show some of his old attitude.

Heathcliff stumbles a little, his legs still a bit weak. I rush over to him, to help him up, and he puts some of his weight on me. He's not light, I can tell you that.

"Can you walk?" I ask him, and he nods.

We take a few steps out of the office and down the stairs of the boathouse. I'm not sure what we ought to do now, since there's a tiger outside, and Heathcliff senses my hesitation.

"Miranda," he says, stopping. He turns his body into mine so we're facing each other.

"Are you okay?" I ask him, my first thought that he might be about to faint again. And I'm definitely sure I can't hold up his whole weight. He's a big boy. Tall and broad.

He just stares at me, intently, and touches my cheek. His dark eyes assess me, drinking in my features as if he hasn't seen me in years. There's something magnetic about those eyes. I can't look away.

The door creaks open then, breaking the spell. We

both turn and look. I fear it'll be the Guardians, having found me, but instead it's two members of the crew team, arriving at the boathouse for their daily practice. There's no point in trying to hide Heathcliff. He's too big to hide. We're caught.

The looks on their faces go from puzzled to worried, as they take in my red vest of shame.

"Dude, that's why the Guardians are swarming the place," one of them says.

I guess the Guardians I ditched outside haven't stopped looking for me.

Not sure quite how to handle the situation, the other pauses awkwardly. Then he recognizes Heathcliff.

"Hey, I *know* you," says one of the crew team members, a look of recognition dawning on his face. "You're that guy. The one who beat up the Guardians last semester."

"Whoa," says another of his teammates. "You're *right*. This is the dude. Heathcliff, right?"

"You don't look so good, man," says the first crew guy. "You okay?"

Heathcliff straightens and nods.

"Why don't we help you back to the dorm?" the other says, taking up Heathcliff's other arm. The other one moves in, as I back away. Neither one acknowledges my presence other than a flittering glance.

"I don't know what kind of brawl you got into, man, but it seems serious," says the other.

"And you," says the other to me. "Unless you want to get us all in trouble, I suggest you head outside first and face those Guardians."

Heathcliff makes a move to stop me, but I stop him with a glance. "It'll be okay," I say. "You let these guys take care of you."

Reluctantly Heathcliff nods. He doesn't like the idea of me leaving him and frankly, I don't, either. I have no other choice.

Outside the boathouse, I run into two Guardians, who look pretty angry. I would be, too, if I had to scour the woods for the last twenty minutes.

"Hi, guys," I say, putting on my sweetest smile. "Miss me?"

Twenty-three

For my little stunt of losing my Guardian guards, I'm held to my room for the remainder of the night, which includes not being able to go to the cafeteria for dinner. Dinner—a messy, lukewarm glob—is delivered on a tray by a Guardian straight to my room. The food, if you want to call it that, is gross, and it makes my room smell vile.

Not to mention, I am dying to get out of here and see how Heathcliff is doing.

I'm relieved on two fronts—one, Heathcliff is alive, and two, there's no way he could be the Hooded Sweatshirt Stalker. It's pretty obvious to me at least that he was too weak to be running around attacking people. He'd been there in that office a long time.

But if I'm honest, the real reason I'm so happy is that he hasn't been ignoring or avoiding me all this time.

And how could I ever doubt him? He didn't abandon me or run away from me. I should've listened to my dreams earlier, I think. I could've saved him weeks ago.

I only hope that those crew boys are taking care of him. Still, Heathcliff is the strongest boy I know. He's probably going to make a fast recovery.

While I dig at my lukewarm dinner, I hear a tapping on my window. Soft at first, and then more insistent. It sounds like a really big moth at first, but I soon realize it's something else. A folded note hangs outside my window. At first I think it's floating there all on its own, but upon closer inspection, I see it's dangling from a fishing line.

I glance over at my door, which has to be kept open (three inches minimum) at all times, so that the Guardian outside can listen for any inappropriate noises, like me trying to make my escape. Then I quietly make my way to my window. The window opens with a creak, which I'm sure will bring the Guardian running. But it doesn't. It's not like I can climb out the window. It's only about four inches across, and a foot high. I gingerly take the note off the fishhook. I recognize the bubbly handwriting immediately—Hana's.

It reads,

Sorry about the low-tech communicado! We think Blake is behind the tiger, but we don't have proof yet. Hang in there. We're trying to clear your name. And any time you want to write us a note, leave it in the copy of *War and Peace,* third from the shelf, at the end of the fourth row in the library, and we'll do the same.

P.S. Use one of your compact mirrors to check us out.

I grab a compact from my drawer and hold it out the window; after a few adjustments, I can see the roof above, and beside a gargoyle, Hana and Blade are leaning out over the edge of the roof, steadying themselves on one of the rooftop gargoyles. They both wave at me. I've never been so glad to see them my whole life.

I wave at them and then I give them the international sign for "wait a minute."

Hurriedly, I rush back to my desk and scribble a note:

Blake is behind this. He kidnapped Heathcliff. Found him in the boathouse. You've got to trust me on this one—he's innocent, I swear. By the way, I LOVE you guys!

I put the note on the hook, and just as the girls reel it in, a Guardian bursts into the room.

"Step away from the window," he commands.

"Can't a girl get some fresh air? My dinner stinks," I say as I step back.

The Guardian looks around suspiciously.

"I may be skinny, but I'm not skinny enough to fit through there," I say, pointing to the narrow window.

He seems to take this under consideration. After glancing around my room once more, he leaves.

I let out a long sigh of relief. When I look out the window again with my compact, I see Blade and Hana are gone.

I reread Hana's note again and this time I notice Blade's also left her mark on it—a crude drawing of some kind of family crest symbol for the LIT society, complete with books and a skull and crossbones.

This makes me smile.

My friends haven't abandoned me. I sit down at my desk and start writing a longer note to leave in the library.

The next morning, I can't wait to get to the library. I whiz through breakfast, anxiously sit through morning assembly, and can barely sit still during first period. My eyes are trained on the slow-moving second hand of the clock above Mr. S's head. Could it move any slower? I head straight to the library at my first opportunity. In my haste to get up the steps, I lose my grip on my notebook and as I swing around to try to catch it, it slips out of my fingers and falls straight at the feet of Ryan Kent.

Of course.

Because this is how I wanted to see him, when I'm wearing my red vest of shame.

"Ryan," I say, startled, and because I've temporarily forgotten that I'm not allowed to speak to anyone.

Ryan automatically stoops down to pick up my notebook and then he hands it to me. There's recognition in Ryan's eyes and something more, I think, before his eyes flick down to my red vest and then back up to my eyes. It looks like he is going to say something. My name, maybe? Or just "hello"? Or "I forgive you for yelling at me at the gym. Why don't we give this boyfriend-girlfriend thing another try?"

But what he wanted to say I'll never know, because as soon as he sees my red vest, he realizes he can't.

And then he turns away from me just as two Guardians come up from behind and stand in front of me, as if to block him from my view. By just handing me my notebook, he could've been punished, but I guess the Guardians aren't in the mood. And technically, he didn't speak to me, so maybe handing me my notebook was a minor offense.

I watch, helplessly, as Ryan walks away from me, down the steps and onto the campus lawn. He never once glances back at me and I watch him until I can't see him anymore.

I glance back up at the Guardians standing near me, but even they don't make eye contact with me. I push past them into the library.

Once inside, I try to refocus on my mission: getting to Hana's latest note. In the copy of *War and Peace,* I find another note from Hana. She writes:

Hi M,

We were skeptical about Heathcliff, but Samir says your story checked out. We think you might be right. I don't know if I can trust Heathcliff yet, but Samir says we can. Apparently, last night Heathcliff saved Samir from being beaten up by a group of hard-core guys on his floor, so Samir is now a fan. I guess we've called a truce with Heathcliff. He really wants to help get you out of figurative expulsion and he seems to be playing nice—for now. He's keeping a low profile so as not to tip off the faculty about him being back. We're working on trying to figure out what to do next. In the meantime, check out aisle 4, row 2 for more info on Blake.

TTFN,

H

Is this possible? Could Heathcliff and Samir, Hana, and Blade have made nice? It's a big leap of faith on Hana's part, so I appreciate it. It's hard to explain how much I know that Heathcliff is innocent this time, but I know I'm right.

I head to the library aisle to read up about Blake.

I discover several things quickly. Blake was born in England in the mid-1700s. He was considered a little eccentric even in his own time, in part because he claimed even then to see angels. He wrote almost exclusively poems about religion, and I read that he was an artist. He was the only poet up until then to illustrate his own works.

I read through everything they have at the library, and before I know it, it's time for mandatory in-room study time. I only make it for a half hour working on my theology paper (it's for Blake, and somehow I'm pretty sure that I'm going to fail) before I need a break.

Bored, I head to my window in hopes of finding another note dangling there, but there is none. The roof is empty. I glance down at the grass, and to the trees beyond, looking for I don't know what.

That's when I see a dark figure standing under my window, leaning against the statute of Shakespeare. Initially I think—Hooded Sweatshirt Stalker! But, in the dim light, I see this person has a head and some rumpled hair. Not the stalker then.

As I watch, he steps out a little into the light, and I see him grab a pack of cigarettes from his jacket pocket and tap one out. The flame from his silver lighter illuminates his face in the dark, giving me a brief glimpse of his nose and stubble and big black eyes before it all goes dark again.

It's Heathcliff.

He's waiting outside my window. How long has he been there?

I wave to him, but he only nods his head once, slowly. I stare at him for a beat or two, before I head back to my desk to finish up my paper.

When I get ready to go to sleep, I still see him outside my window.

He's there, leaning against the same tree, the light of his cigarette burning red in the dark.

Twenty-four

Heathcliff knows better than to talk to me, for fear of raising Guardian suspicion, but he does follow me at a discreet distance throughout the next couple of days. I feel a lot less lonely, knowing he's there, and he takes up a permanent vigil outside my window at night. The boy apparently doesn't need sleep.

On Friday after dinner I notice, however, that he isn't at his usual post. I wonder what this means, when I hear a strange sound coming from across campus.

It takes me a moment to realize the sound is actually music.

The spring break dance! I'd completely forgotten. I strain to try to pick out the song, but I can only really hear a bass beat. It's so weird to hear music again after not hearing it for months.

I have a sudden flash of what I'm missing: the gym decorated in streamers and banners; a DJ spinning songs; Samir and Hana finally hooking up by making out in a dark corner; Parker manhandling Ryan on the dance floor; Blade and her new date doing a swing dance, whirling around in the middle of the gym. And for once—no school uniforms. Everyone is in silk and satin. I should be glad I'm missing it, but I'm not. Being the campus pariah totally sucks.

That's when there's a new sound at my door that has nothing to do with music. It's a loud thump, followed by a thud. When I rush to the hall, I see the Guardian who's normally standing there crumpled in a heap at my feet.

Above him is Heathcliff, fists clenched at his sides in a fighting stance.

Before I even think twice about it, I throw my arms around his neck and hug him. It's like hugging a wall, he's that broad and tall.

"You've come to save me!" I say, stating the obvious.

"Duh," Hana says, stepping out from behind Heathcliff. Samir is with her, too.

"So you and Heathcliff really are friends now."

"Not exactly friends, but working on it," Hana says.

"Come on, we don't have much time," Samir says. "Everyone is at the dance. Now's our chance."

Both Samir and Hana are not in uniform. They're wearing what look like party clothes. Samir is in a suit without a tie, and Hana is wearing a purple silk sleeveless dress, which doesn't exactly go with her black-framed glasses, but oh, well. I have to introduce that girl to contacts one of these days.

Even Heathcliff is looking dressier than usual. He's got on a white shirt, loosened at the collar, and a black blazer. All he's missing is the cumberbund and the bow tie and he'd be in a tux. His dark, thick hair is ruffled, but in a perfectly ruffled kind of way. And he's sporting his trademark stubble.

"Our chance for what?" I ask. "To slow dance?"

"To clear your name—hello!" Hana says, grabbing me by the arm and pushing me back into my room. "But first, you need to change."

"Wow—nice!" Samir says when we emerge about ten minutes later. I'm wearing my only formal dress—a peach-colored chiffon halter dress—with my hair thrown up in a messy bun, and enough smoky eye shadow so that even my own mother might not recognize me. But then again, that's the point. I'm supposed to be in disguise. Besides, I'm showing off enough leg so most people probably won't be looking at my face. In fact, Heathcliff is staring at a spot just above my knees. When he catches me looking at him, he flushes, ever so slightly. I guess that means he approves.

"So are we going to sit around all day staring at Miranda's legs, or are we going to get busy snooping?" Hana asks.

"Legs?" Samir asks tentatively.

"Wrong answer, you goof," Hana says, smacking Samir with her satin evening handbag.

Hana and Samir take us to Macduff dorm, where Blake is supposed to live. The entire dorm is empty, like most of the rest of campus, since pretty much everyone is at the dance. This includes Blake, who is acting as one of the dance chaperones, as well as most of the Guardians, who are on double duty making sure the large gathering doesn't turn violent. With this crew of delinquents, it's always a possibility.

Heathcliff enters Blake's room first, making sure the coast is clear. When he signals us in, I expect to find a typical faculty room—mostly bare, with lots of books, and no bed. Instead, I find myself standing in a room covered from floor to ceiling in drawings. Drawings of angels and devils. Of men, and lambs, and tigers.

"But how are the drawings related to the real tiger?" Hana asks, getting close enough to one of the tiger pictures to rub her hand down its edge. "Is he bringing the tiger alive somehow with the sketches?"

"Um, guys, look at these," Samir says, pointing to one wall. It's covered in pictures of hell. Gruesome, vivid pictures of bodies being torn limb from limb and demons eating pieces of flesh. In other words: serious ick factor.

Heathcliff frowns at the pictures as he takes a step closer to them.

"Looks like something Blade would like," Hana says.

"I don't know about that," I say. "These might be even too gross for her. Speaking of Blade, where is she?"

"At the dance," Samir says. "She's keeping an eye on Blake for us. Make sure he stays put."

"Yeah, it's not exactly a rough assignment," Hana says. "If you ask me, she just didn't want to miss her slow dance with Number Thirty-one."

I glance back at Heathcliff to see if he's listening, but he's moved forward to the wall of grossness and is peeling back one of the drawings. Soon he rips it down completely. He grabs another and another, tearing them all down.

"Hey! What are you doing!" Samir cries.

But Heathcliff doesn't stop, he takes down enough pictures until we see the wall beneath, which shows a little door, Heathcliff pushes on the door and it swings open. Another hidden passageway. Just like the one in Ms. W's room.

"How did you know that was there?" Hana asks Heathcliff, who shrugs.

"The pictures," he says, pointing to the hellish ones, "are supposed to encourage people to stay away from his wall."

I can see his point. I certainly don't want to look too closely at a demon gnawing on a man's leg.

Hana gives Heathcliff a look of grudging admiration. Heathcliff may not read much (or barely at all), but he's definitely not dumb.

Heathcliff grabs an unlit torch from the wall and lights it with a silver lighter from his pocket. He offers me a torch, too, and I take it as I follow him into the dark passageway.

"Um, guys, we're not actually *going* in here?" Samir asks, even as Hana follows us. "Guys? I don't think that's a good idea."

After a few seconds, though, we hear the patter of Samir's feet. "For the record, this is a *terrible* idea," he says.

"Just be quiet, and quit stepping on my heels!" Hana hisses at him.

Along the way, Heathcliff lights other torches and hands them back to us, so we're each carrying one. The torchlight flickers against the walls, throwing shadows along the narrow hallway. I move close to Heathcliff, taking hold of the back of his shirt so that he doesn't lose me in the dark. Instinctively he turns and grabs my hand with his, holding it tight as he moves forward into the darkness. His hand is big and strong and comforting. I instantly feel calmer.

Something small and black flies by our heads then. It looks like it might be a bat. It's followed by one or two more. Suddenly Samir shouts "Dracula!"

Heathcliff rolls me over against the wall, as if protecting me from whatever it is. By the time we realize it's not Dracula at all, but just a couple of loose bats, the wall gives way behind me, spinning us both around into a tiny storage room. Our torches have gone out in the struggle. Heathcliff fumbles in his pocket and picks out his lighter. He flicks it on and the small room is illuminated. I see a couple of boxes, and on top of them—a hooded sweatshirt. And not just any sweatshirt. *The* sweatshirt. From Headless Sweatshirt Stalker Guy. I pick it up and show Heathcliff, who nods slowly.

"We have to find a way out," he tells me. With barely enough room for us both to stand, Heathcliff feels around us for the trigger that opened the door. He reaches his arm across me and suddenly, I feel the extreme closeness of him, the strangeness of our situation completely leaving my head, as I feel the warmth of his breath on my ear.

Heathcliff glances down at me and notices me looking at him. The flickering flame from his lighter casts shadows along his face, but I can see his eyes. They're dark and unreadable.

He stops searching for an exit and stares at me a long while, and I realize that I'm alone with Heathcliff in close quarters. My heart starts to speed up just a little. And just as I start to wonder if he's going to kiss me, he leans in, draws me closer to him, and covers my lips with his.

I'm momentarily stunned, and not just because a strange boy is kissing me, in a hidden passageway, while we're stuck in a closet. But from the sheer electricity of his lips on mine. There are enough volts in this kiss to power my hair dryer and more. It's like— *POW!*—I'm seeing stars.

Every other thought I've ever had leaves my head and there's just me and Heathcliff, with his lips on mine. And a small voice in my head tells me Ryan never kissed me like this.

And the world seems to be spinning and I realize belatedly because it is. The door to the secret closet is spinning again, and suddenly Heathcliff and I are back out into the hallway, with Hana and Samir staring at us.

Hana gives us a stern and disapproving look.

"Um, I hate to interrupt you *love birds,* but we've got an insane teacher to catch, or don't you remember?"

My face feels red and I don't know if it's because

I'm embarrassed, or because Heathcliff had such an effect on me, but I blubber, "We found the sweatshirt—from the stalker—in there."

"Let's see," Hana says, pulling on one of the wall torches. She lets it go, just as the wall-door is halfway open, so we can easily go in and out. The torchlight from the passageway illuminates the storage room.

"Look, the vault books," Hana says grabbing *For Whom the Bell Tolls* and *To the Lighthouse* from an open box. They're Coach H and Ms. W's books—the ones that hold their souls. She whips open the covers. But unlike last semester, when I freed them by opening their books, this time no Coach H or Ms. W appear.

"Am I doing something wrong?" Hana asks me.

"I don't know. Let me see," I say. I do the same thing, and again, nothing happens. I flip through the books and that's when I notice there are pages missing from each of them. They've been ripped out.

"That's why they don't work," I say, holding up the ripped-out edge for Hana to see.

"Okay, um, I think we have a bigger problem," Samir says, holding up the drawing that he found underneath the books. He shows it to us. It depicts the school gym, decorated for a dance, and filled with students. Only there's a giant tiger in the middle of the dance floor, clawing at a student. Above the tiger's head, there's a single word: Judgment.

Twenty-five

The four of us sprint out of the closet and into the secret passageway.

"Which way?" Samir asks.

"Back to the boys' dorm," Hana says, starting to head back in the direction we'd come.

"Wait," Heathcliff says, holding up a hand. "I think it's faster this way."

He leads us on and trips one of the torchlights, opening yet another door. This one leads into Ms. W's room.

"How did you know this was here?" Hana asks, suddenly wary.

"Lucky guess," Heathcliff says, walking through the door.

Hana gives me a sharp look, as if to tell me she doesn't believe him.

"We don't have time to argue," I say. "We've got a dance to save."

The four of us sprint to the gym, just as the chapel clock chimes 8:00 P.M.

"The dance is over soon," Hana gasps, out of breath. "If he hasn't acted now, he will soon."

We slow down our pace near the doors of the gym, where four Guardians are standing watch. Hana, however, marches ahead with Samir in tow, and Heathcliff and I follow, making sure not to make eye contact. The four of us walk by the Guardians like we belong there, and they let us pass. Hana was right about dressing the part—we look like any other dancegoers, and they don't stop us.

The gym is decorated with pastel yellow and blue paper streamers, and there's a giant papier-mâché daisy hanging down from the center of the rafters. I wonder how long Parker and her clones worked on that. Then I realize they probably just bribed someone to do it for them.

The dance floor is crowded with kids, and the tones of Coldplay drift out over their heads. There are colored lights shining down and the place looks more like a dance club than a school. I search the crowd frantically for any signs of Blake, but find none.

The song on the floor changes from Coldplay to

Death Cab for Cutie. It's the same song that Ryan played on our first date. I suddenly feel like I'm going to be sick.

I tell myself this is no time to throw myself a pity party. I've got to think about finding Blake.

Around us, couples are forming on the dance floor and swaying back and forth in time with the music. I don't see either Blade or Number Thirty-one. But I do see Ryan Kent, and he's dancing, body-to-body, with none other than Parker Rodham.

"Uh-oh," Hana says, nudging me.

She nods her head toward Derek Mann about thirty feet from us. He's talking to a couple of Guardians and pointing at me. The rat! The Guardians look up and nod, and it seems like they're making their way for us. We're sitting ducks.

"Come on," I say, taking Heathcliff's hand and heading straight into the sea of people on the dance floor.

Hana and Samir place themselves in the path of the Guardians, so they can't quite get to us, and before I can even think about whether or not Heathcliff can dance, he's got his arm around me, and is expertly leading me in small circles.

For a second, I completely forget about Blake and the Guardians trying to get to us in the crowd, as Heathcliff's arm tightens around the back of my waist, and he pulls me to him. He actually *knows* how to dance.

"I don't know the steps," I stutter, suddenly feeling awkward in his arms.

"You don't have to know them," Heathcliff says, and he steers me around in a circle. It's true. He's leading. I just have to follow. He's strong and firm and yet surprisingly graceful. Heathcliff is full of surprises. I look up at his face and he's staring at me intently. His black eyes are so big and deep, I feel like I'm a little lost in them. They're hypnotizing. Under his gaze, I feel my face grow hot.

"Aren't we supposed to look for Blake?" I ask him.

Reluctantly, Heathcliff pulls his gaze from me and sweeps the gym. I do the same as he steers me expertly through the crowd.

And then, suddenly, another couple collides into us, sending me straight into Heathcliff's chest. I pull away in time to see that couple is Ryan and Parker.

"I'm sorry . . ." Ryan starts, and then he sees me. He looks up and sees Heathcliff, too, and the apology dries up on his tongue. He gets a hard look on his face.

"I guess they let *just anybody* in—that is, if you actually *were allowed* in," Parker snarls at me. "Come on, Ry. I smell something bad over here."

Ry? She has a nickname for him and it's "Ry"? Like rye bread? That's the dumbest thing I've ever heard. Ryan is not a name that could benefit from shortening.

Parker gives me an evil look over Ryan's shoulder.

Under normal circumstances I would consider clawing Parker's eyes out, but over her shoulder, I get a glimpse of Blake.

"There!" I cry to Heathcliff. "He's over there."

Heathcliff zeroes in on where I'm looking, and in seconds takes off through the crowd without another thought. I try to follow him, but the crowd is too thick and I quickly fall behind.

Even worse, I bump straight into Derek Mann, who puts both his hands on my shoulders and stops my forward progress.

"Hey there, hot stuff, where are you going in such a hurry? Looks like you need a dance partner," he says.

"Let me *go*," I shout at him, trying to wriggle past him as I watch Heathcliff close the distance between us and Blake, who is running fast to the far doors of the gym.

"What's your hurry?"

"You 'tell' on me to the Guardians, and you don't understand why I don't want to spend any time with you? Are you dumb *and* stupid or just dumb?"

Derek actually pauses to consider this as if it's a real question. But before he can come to an answer, the lights above us go out and the music stops.

There's some nervous laughter. "What the hell?" I hear someone near me say.

"Is this your idea of getting me alone in the dark?" Derek jokes next to me.

"Shut up, Derek," I say, giving him a hard shove with my elbow. Next to me, I hear him go "*ooof*."

"Stay calm," shouts a teacher. There's more laughter and someone does a spooky ghost sound: "Ooooooooooh." This is followed by more laughs.

The backup generator lights go on then. They're much dimmer than the overhead lights, and they're mostly above the exit doors. They shine pools of light into the center of the gym, spotlighting different couples and groups of students, but leaving many of us in shadow.

Heathcliff is moving toward me through the crowd, a look of urgency on his face.

"We've got to leave," he shouts to me and adds something I can't quite hear.

"Heathcliff . . ." I get out, just as he reaches us and grabs my arm. He squeezes it a little too hard. "Hey, what—"

"We need to leave, *now*," Heathcliff thunders, leaving no room for argument.

And then there's a loud *clang*, as the gym doors on the south end, the ones without working spotlights, bang open. The noise temporarily silences Heathcliff. It silences the whole gym. Everyone's eyes go to the south doors. Something is moving through them. Something big and shadowy.

"It's a cougar!" someone shouts. But I know it's not a cougar. It's something much bigger. It's Blake's tiger.

A few people shriek and start running from the door. The animal itself moves slowly, almost languidly, inside, avoiding all direct light.

"That's too big to be a cougar," someone near me whispers.

The animal moves into one spotlight, showing its orange-and-black stripes. Now everyone can see it's a tiger. People in front of it scatter. There are a few muffled shouts. Behind us, I see Derek Mann hide behind a girl half his size, and then nearly throw her into the path of the animal while he runs the other way. Nice. I can see he's as brave in times of trouble as I would've thought.

"Everyone exit the gym in an orderly fashion," I hear Headmaster B shout, as Guardians cautiously approach the tiger with their hands up, trying to contain it.

There's a rush, not yet a panic, of people moving to the doors. We're swept up in the flow of people.

I glance backward, over my shoulder, and see bits and pieces. A tail. A paw. Odds and ends exposed by the light as it walks, almost casually, into the gym. It moves like it's half panther, half wolf, with the size of two of each put together.

Partly in shadow, partly in light, its eyes glow red in the flicker of the emergency lights. It bears its fangs to the dancers and gives a low growl. A few students gasp and the rest move away from it, some quickly, some slowly. The Guardians close in on it, encircling it, in an ever-tightening ring. But while the Guardians may intimidate the students, they don't seem to be scaring the tiger very much. He glances around at the four of them, and bares its fangs a little. The Guardians lose their nerve, glancing at one another uneasily. Sensing their hesitation, the tiger pounces. It knocks one of them flat on his back, clawing at his head. And then, as if losing interest in him, it takes off at a bounding run, right toward us. Before I know it, it's jumped into the thickest part of the crowd moving toward the exit.

There's a blood-curdling scream. And after that, everyone scatters.

Twenty-six

In the confusion and the dark, Heathcliff pulls me behind him as I scramble blindly toward the exit, along with the other two hundred or so kids moving in the same direction. Heathcliff is holding my hand, when I hear someone calling Ryan's name.

It's Parker, and she's fallen near the refreshment table and is having trouble getting up. Everyone else is too busy trying to get away to help her. The tiger leaps upon a freshman boy's back, twenty feet from Parker. They both scream, and Parker tries to slide away from the tiger on her butt and hands.

And then I see Ryan run over to try to help Parker up.

"Wait," I tell Heathcliff, whipping my hand loose as I skid to a stop and change direction.

"Miranda!" he shouts, as the crowd comes between

us. He frantically tries to back through it, even as I'm moving toward Ryan.

Around us, the faculty members are frozen to the spot. They're unsure of what to do, especially in front of all the students. None of them wants to show their powers in front of the whole school.

And then I see the tiger. It's eyeing Ryan and Parker. It loses interest in the freshman it has pinned underneath one paw and starts to inch forward toward the refreshment table, and Ryan.

But neither Ryan, nor Parker, see the big cat, or how very close it's getting to them. They have their backs to it, as Ryan helps Parker to her feet. She's holding her ankle and limping. The tiger is coming up behind them, closer now, with its legs tense and its hindquarters coiled, as if it's ready to pounce.

"Ryan! Look out!" I shout, even as I realize there's no way they'll be able to get away in time. Suddenly desperate to get the big cat's attention, I grab one of the silver streamers from above my head and jump up on the bleachers nearby. I stomp my foot loudly against the metal bleachers and wave the strand of silver under the emergency light, hoping that tigers are like big tabby cats—easily distracted by shiny things.

My ploy works. In fact, it works *too* well.

The tiger transfers its attention from Ryan and

Parker straight to me. I drop the streamer and start running crossways down the bleachers, hoping to elude the tiger, but it's too fast. It makes a leap, and at the last minute I scrunch myself down in between the bleachers, falling about three feet to the ground below. I hear the tiger land heavily on the bleachers above me, and a paw comes down, through the cracks in the benches above, and just whips through my hair.

Talk about a serious bad hair day.

As I'm trying to figure out what to do next, two strong arms grab me and pull me backward. They belong to Heathcliff.

"Come on," he says.

This time I don't argue.

"We have to try to run for the door," Heathcliff tells me. This means running out from the bleachers for about ten feet to a swinging door.

"We're not going to make it," I say.

"We have to try," Heathcliff says. "Ready? Let's go."

Heathcliff sprints forward, tugging on my arm and making me run a lot faster than I think I can go. Out of the corner of my eye I see the tiger, or at least a big shadowy blob following us, running down the bleachers and getting ready to make a leap toward us. My legs are pumping hard. Heathcliff and I make it to the door just as the tiger leaps over us, slamming itself into the door frame, blocking our exit. Heathcliff falls on purpose, sliding beneath the animal, and he takes me with him. We skid on the ground, gliding to a halt just a few feet on the other side of the tiger.

I can almost feel the heat of its breath. Smells worse than Derek Mann's.

"Nice kitty?" I squeak. "Sit? Stay?"

The tiger just snarls, curling its lip even more.

Heathcliff pushes me behind him as he scrambles to his feet.

"Here! Over here, Garfield!" cries Ryan. He's banging a folding chair against the bleachers to get its attention. Distracted by the noise, it looks up. Seeing Ryan, it runs away from us.

I watch in nearly slow motion as the tiger leaps into Ryan, knocking him flat. Ryan falls to the ground, hitting his head on the bleachers as he goes, and lies very still. "Ryan!" I shout, but he doesn't move. The tiger lifts its paw as if to strike him with its claws, but before it can land a blow, Headmaster B has whacked it across the snout with a folding chair. The tiger reels backward, whimpering. Still smarting from the blow, it shakes its head and then runs back into the corner of the gym, where it's hidden in shadow.

"We've got to go," Heathcliff says, dragging me to my feet and pushing me out the door.

"But Ryan. We can't leave him."

"The tiger may come back, and we can't help him

now," Heathcliff says, tugging on my arm and making sure I can't get away.

The last thing I see before Heathcliff pulls me out of the gym is Parker bending over Ryan's body, gently placing her hand on his forehead.

"Let me go," I shout, twisting away from Heathcliff's grip, but he just tightens his hold.

"Listen to me," he says, "we have to find Blake to get to the bottom of this or more people will be hurt."

"He has a point," Hana says, as she and Samir join us in the crowd milling about outside the gym.

"Can we hurry up and discuss this somewhere not out in the open where a giant man-eating tiger might attack us?" Samir asks, glancing around nervously.

"Wait, there he is," Hana says, pointing across the campus lawn. A shadowy figure is running toward the chapel.

"The tiger? Where!" shouts Samir, sounding panicked.

"No, not the tiger, you goof, *Blake*."

"You're sure that's Blake?"

"It's him," Heathcliff says, starting to move in that direction. Hana, Samir, and I follow.

Inside the chapel is dark and the pews are empty. I don't see where Blake has gone. It's like he's disappeared into thin air.

"We should split up," Heathcliff says. "Miranda and

I will take the lower level. You both take the upstairs."

"How about let's *not* split up," Samir says, crossing his arms across his chest in protest. "If this were a movie, I'd be the nerdy guy who gets killed off first. Yeah, no thanks."

"Samir, *come on*," Hana whispers, dragging him away by the arm. "I'll protect you, you sissy."

"I'm not a sissy. I am being *practical*," Samir says. "I mean, who do you think that tiger is going to eat first. Me or Heathcliff? Yeah, I thought so."

"We're after Blake, not the tiger," Hana hisses at him, and they argue all the way up the stairs to the balcony level.

"Not exactly stealth, are they?" I ask Heathcliff, who just quirks an eyebrow at me. It might be my imagination, but I think there's the beginning of a smile on his face.

Just as quickly as the near-smile comes, it's gone, replaced by a look of determination as Heathcliff takes my hand and leads the way down the side aisle of the chapel. His hand is big and strong and dry, and mine fits almost entirely inside his palm, as if it were meant to be there.

Heathcliff tightens his grip on my hand and pulls me a little closer.

Around us and above us are the stained glass scenes from famous Shakespeare plays. *Romeo and*

Juliet. Hamlet. Macbeth. From the pictures here, Shakespeare was sure fond of swordfights. Dim light from the campus streetlamps outside filter into the church, casting colored shadows on the floor near our feet.

There's a slight grinding sound above us. Heathcliff freezes, putting out his arm to protect me. But when we both look up, all I see is the large pane of glass, where an oversize Hamlet has his sword drawn. The window is intact and still.

We take another step and I hear the sound again, this time louder. On the floor, the colored shadow seems to be shifting. I tug on Heathcliff's arm, but he already seems to know what's happening, because he pushes me out of harm's way and into a pew, where I stumble and then catch myself on the back of a bench. When I glance back, it looks like the glass window is falling on Heathcliff, but then I realize it's not falling. It's *jumping*. Hamlet, complete with sword, has come to life, and he seems intent on fighting Heathcliff.

Hamlet is made of glass, and he seems to be on the flat side, but when he brings down his sword, it slices through the edge of the pew, sending a chunk of wood flying off. Heathcliff jumps back, his eyes wide, as he looks around for a weapon.

"Up here," Samir shouts, from the balcony above Heathcliff. He throws down an umbrella that he found who knows where. Heathcliff catches it and then gives it a doubtful look. Hamlet rushes him, however, leaving Heathcliff no choice but to try to deflect a sword with a Mary Poppins umbrella. He manages to fend off two attacks, but I can tell that umbrella isn't going to hold up much longer. I scan the church for anything sharp, and my eyes land on the metal replica of a giant quill pen at the front of the chapel. It's sitting in an oversize fake well of ink, and I wonder if it comes loose.

When I run to it and give it a good yank, it falls freely into my hands. It's slightly smaller than the umbrella, but the point is sharper and it's made of pewter, which has to be better than the aluminum frame of the umbrella. While I run to help Heathcliff, Samir shouts, and I whirl to see that above me on the balcony Lady Macbeth has come to life, and is chasing Samir and Hana around with her outstretched, blood-drenched hands. They run, dodging her attacks. They try to slow her down by throwing Bard Academy hymn books at her.

I can't stop, though, I have to get the metal quill to Heathcliff. Across the chapel, I see Hamlet slice straight through the umbrella. Heathcliff throws the pieces at the glass figure, which bounce off Hamlet without doing any damage.

"Heathcliff!" I shout, tossing the quill pen as I do so. He whips around, catching it just in time to deflect another blow. The sword lands with a hard clink against the metal pen. For a second, Heathcliff and Hamlet struggle for dominance, each one pushing hard against the other. It's Hamlet that finally budges, taking a step backward. Heathcliff takes advantage of Hamlet's off-balanced footing and shoves him hard. Hamlet trips over the corner of the pew and falls. While he's on his back, Heathcliff runs the metal quill pen straight through his middle, breaking the glass. The point, buried in the stone floor, traps Hamlet by his metal rims, lashing him fast to the ground. Heathcliff quickly kicks the sword out of Hamlet's hand.

Heathcliff, sweaty and a bit out of breath, steps back and wipes his forehead. That's when another glass pane above us wiggles to life. This one is Macduff, I think, because he whips his sword out of Macbeth and crawls out of the window. Uh-oh. Not good.

"Heathcliff! Behind you," I shout.

Heathcliff looks up in time just to avoid being stomped on by Macduff. He manages to knock Macbeth's sword away, and then the two of them become locked in a hand-to-hand struggle.

On the balcony above us, I see Blake, who's peeking up over the railing. When he sees me, he quickly ducks back down.

I take to the stairs two at a time, trying to get up to Blake.

"Miranda! Wait!" Heathcliff shouts at me. His forward momentum, however, is cut off by the attacking Macduff, who hits him hard, sending him whirling backward. "Heathcliff!" I shout, stopping on the stairs, holding my breath. Then I see Heathcliff stand up from behind a pew and shake his head, as if to recover. He gives me a sheepish look and then refocuses his attention on Macduff. His brow furrowed, he grabs the nearest weapon—Hamlet's sword—and charges at Macduff.

At the top of the stairs, I nearly get hit with a flying hymnal flung by Samir who, along with Hana, is still battling Lady Macbeth. I run past them, toward the front of the balcony where I saw Blake, and I find him, crouched between pews, furiously rolling up rubbings he's made of the stained glass windows. So this is how he did it! He's made drawings of them and somehow he's making the drawings come to life.

"Blake!" I cry. "Stop this, now!" As if he'd listen to me.

"Gabriele says I mustn't," Blake says, tucking a roll of paper under his arm. "Have you seen this church? It's a sacrilege. A church with no homage to the Holy Trinity. It's God's will that it be destroyed. Gabriele says so."

"What are you talking about?"

"Gabriele has told me that God wants Bard Academy destroyed. It's a blight on His name."

Okay, I think Blake has officially wandered over from the Eccentric Artist Camp to the Insane/World Domination Camp. Now he thinks God wants him to destroy Bard Academy?

I glance down at Blake's coat and see a torn book with pages sticking out. Could it be the missing pages from *For Whom the Bell Tolls* or *To the Lighthouse*? I'm betting so.

"Wait one second. Let's talk about this," I say, trying to stall for time while I think of a way to get those pages from him.

While Blake talks, I see below us that Heathcliff is getting the upper hand in his fight with Macduff. Heathcliff punches the glass figure in the face, cracking the stained glass around his nose and sending him back a few paces. While off-balance, Heathcliff whips his foot around, sweeping the legs out from under Macduff. And then, with his bare hands, Heathcliff breaks off Macduff's legs at the knees, and for good measure pins him to the ground underneath a pew. Talk about serious bad-boy mojo.

"Blake, give me the pages. It's over now," I say.

Blake glances from one side to the other. I take a step forward, and he takes a step back. I'm not sure how I'm going to make him give me those pages, but I know I have to try.

That's when something strange starts to happen.

Blake, isn't, well, *Blake.* He starts to transform before my eyes, from the pudgy, far-from-intimidating theology teacher into the tiger that terrorized us all in the gym. The clothes Blake was wearing fall to the floor in a heap, along with the pages from Coach H and Ms. W's books. His drawings, too, fall to the ground.

My heart is thumping in my chest as I take in the sheer *giantness* of the big cat. Its paws are the size of dinner plates. I'm pretty sure my entire face would fit in its jaws. As soon as I think that, I shudder.

The tiger bares its fangs at me, and leaps.

Twenty-seven

I brace for the impact of a four-hundred-pound cat, but instead I'm whisked away in the nick of time and the tiger lands on the pew behind me, breaking it into two halves. I blink and realize that it's Heathcliff who's saved me. He's got both arms around me and we're lying on the floor, face-to-face.

"I told you you should've waited for me," Heathcliff says. He's got the beginnings of a smile at the corners of his mouth.

Behind us, Samir shouts, "Okay! How is this fair? We have to deal with the tiger, too?"

Heathcliff and I sit up and see Samir and Hana cornered by both Lady Macbeth and the tiger. We look at each other and Heathcliff pulls himself to his feet. He takes the sword that he'd been using to fight Macduff and throws it like a spear straight at the tiger. It nips the tiger, slicing through the end of its tail. Annoyed, the tiger flicks its head toward us.

Now it's really peeved.

It growls and starts toward us, and I back away, my foot catching on one of Blake's drawings on the floor. I slip a little, ripping the edge of one of the tiger drawings. In front of us, the tiger yelps, as if we'd hurt it.

"The drawing!" I hiss to Heathcliff. Understanding dawning on his face, he grinds his own heel into the picture, tearing it a little more, and causing the tiger to yelp again and back away from us. Then, as if deciding it can't fight us, the tiger turns around and leaps off the balcony, landing on the floor below with graceful skill. It disappears under us, and then we hear it bang through the front chapel door.

Heathcliff moves to follow it, but before he can, we hear Samir shout, "Uh, a little help back here?"

I turn and see that he's been pinned down by Lady Macbeth and Hana is struggling to get her off.

"We've got to help them," I say, even as Heathcliff is already springing into action. He grabs Lady Macbeth by the neck, but she wiggles free from him, sliding a dagger around and slicing through Heathcliff's sleeve. I see a thin trail of blood where her glass blade swiped him.

And just as Heathcliff struggles to get her back into control, another figure leaps up to the balcony. It's

Macduff. He's somehow freed himself from the pew and is now back for round two. I pick up the folding chair and try to spar with him, but he knocks it easily out of my hand and sends me skidding across the floor on my hip.

"Miranda!" I hear Heathcliff shout in a panic.

The next thing I know I've come to a hard stop against a pew. Serious ouch. I'm pretty sure that's going to leave a bruise.

"Miranda! Are you okay?" This from Hana, who's come over to see if she can help. I glance up and see Samir trying to get Lady Macbeth off Heathcliff's back. She's pulling on his hair and screeching.

Samir, however, keeps getting knocked backward by her flailing arms.

It doesn't take a genius to figure out that we're losing this battle. Suddenly Heathcliff puts his arms on Lady Macbeth and flings her, hard, off his back, sending her colliding into Macduff in a smash of glass and iron. The two figures get temporarily entangled with each other on the ground. They roll together, trying to get up.

"Can you stand?" Hana asks me, a worried look on her face.

Still dazed, I nod. I try to get up, but I'm sitting on a heap of Blake's drawings and they're slippery.

"Wait! The drawings," I say, betting that the tiger

and the glass figures probably have the same kind of kryptonite: Blake's drawings. "We need to rip them up," I tell Hana.

The glass figures of Macbeth and Macduff have now disentangled themselves from each other and are preparing to make another attack on Heathcliff and Samir. Heathcliff steadies himself by grabbing hold of a nearby folding chair. Samir stands behind Heathcliff, using him as a human shield.

I grab at the first drawing I see, Macduff. I tear it in two pieces. I glance up just in time to see that the stained glass version of Macduff seems to lose his arm. It simply falls off and clanks on the floor.

Hana drops to the floor beside me, and together we rip up every drawing we can find. Behind us, Macduff clatters to the floor in pieces. Lady Macbeth lunges again at Heathcliff, just as I find her drawing at the bottom of the stack. She shoves Heathcliff out of the way and heads right for Samir, her dagger raised. Samir cringes and shuts both eyes tightly, preparing for the blow. I rip up her drawing and she falls in a heap at Samir's feet.

After a second or two, Samir tentatively opens one eye and then the other. Seeing the heap of Lady Mac-Beth at his feet, he cries, "Yeah, *that's* what I'm talking about! Watch who you're messing with."

Hana and I look at each other, but decide to say

nothing. If Samir wants to think he vanquished Lady Macbeth, that's fine by me. Samir kicks Lady Macbeth's broken pieces, but then winces with pain. "Ow," he cries, holding his foot.

"Heathcliff! Your hands," I cry, looking at his bleeding knuckles. He must've gotten cut from the stained glass figures. I take his right hand in mine and bind it with my Bard necktie. Heathcliff winces a little, but then gives me a grateful look.

"I hate to break this Hallmark moment, but look what I found," Hana says, picking up a couple of old book pages. The text at the bottom of each page tells us they're the missing pages from *To the Lighthouse* and *For Whom the Bell Tolls.*

I hand Hana the books from the passageway. I watch as she replaces the missing pages with the ones Blake left behind.

"Step back everybody," Hana says. "Here comes backup."

The pages fuse back together on their own, and as soon as the books are complete, Ms. W and Coach H emerge, whole, from both of them.

"That's about time," Ms. W says, giving me a smile.

"What took you so long?" Coach H growls, snatching the books from my hands. "Do you have any idea how *cramped* it is in there?"

"And by the way, you're welcome," Samir says.

"Wait a blasted minute," Coach H says, taking in Heathcliff for the first time. "Just what is *he* doing here?"

"He's on our side," I say.

"Is this true?" Ms. W asks Hana and Samir. They both nod.

"A temporary truce then," Ms. W says, eyeing Heathcliff warily.

"Emphasis on the temporary," Coach H adds.

"So do we have any idea how to catch this guy?" Samir asks.

"I think I may have an idea," Ms. W says.

We all lean forward to listen.

Ms. W believes that Blake thinks he's on a mission from God. That he's taken the form of a tiger is significant, because the tiger to Blake represents the proof of God's power. The poem itself discusses how the creator of the tiger has to be more fierce and powerful than the creature itself. He's found a way, Ms. W says, of bringing to life characters in his mind *without* the help of the books from the vault. And based on what we found in his room and in the secret passageway, she thinks he plans on trying to conjure angels and other characters he believes will bring about the Apocalypse.

"There we go, end of the world again," Samir says.

"How come it's always the end of the world as we know it? Why doesn't anyone want world domination? What kind of bad guys *are* these?"

"Blake doesn't think he's bad," Hana says. "He thinks he's doing the right thing."

"But where is he hiding?" Coach H asks.

"He would want to be on what he thinks is holy ground," Hana says. "To do what he thinks he has to do."

"The old church," Ms. W whispers.

"Old church?"

"Before the chapel was built, Bard Academy had an old church. It's where the boathouse is now. You can still see its foundation, next to where the boathouse was built."

"My dream!" I exclaim. "So that explains why I was dreaming about a church all this time."

"It burned down in 1847, when much of the campus burned in the great fire," Coach H says.

"Hey, that was the same year that *Wuthering Heights* was published. That's when Heathcliff came into being," Hana says. Heathcliff scowls at her and Hana hastily adds, "Not, of course, that you had anything to do with the fire."

"That we know of," Ms. W adds.

"Frankenstein was responsible, or so legend has it," Coach H adds.

"So Blake would've know about the church, be-cause he was here *before* 1847," Hana says.

"That's right," Ms. W says, nodding.

"What are we waiting for?" I ask.

"Wait, we're going to go into the woods *now*?" Samir asks. "Do I need to remind you people that it's dark out. *And* there's a tiger on the loose?"

"Don't be such a sissy," Hana says, poking Samir in the ribs.

"Maybe Samir's right," Ms. W says. "Maybe it isn't right for you children to come along."

"Hey," I say, "we rescued *you,* remember? You can't let us sit this one out."

Reluctantly, Ms. W and Coach H agree.

Twenty-eight

We make it down the path to the boathouse, which is nearly dark, except for the subtle glow surrounding Ms. W and Coach H. As ghosts, apparently, they can glow when they feel like it, which is one of the many odd side effects of being dead.

"Have you guys ever thought of going to a rave? You guys are like walking glow sticks," Samir says.

"Raves? Who goes to raves anymore?" I ask Samir.

"I'm just saying, these guys would be popular on the DJ circuit," Samir says.

"As if you even *know* what a DJ circuit is," Hana scoffs.

"What's a DJ?" Coach H asks us, looking puzzled. Naturally, one of the downsides of being dead is that you're not exactly up to speed on current events. It's like being lame and clueless for eternity.

"*Shhhhhh*," Ms. Woolf warns as we get closer to the boathouse. The boathouse is dark, but as Ms. Woolf steps forward, the glow surrounding her sheds light on the horseshoe-shaped tree and the giant boulder, and in between them, what's left of the foundation of the old chapel.

Behind us, on the path, comes the distinctive low growl of the tiger.

"Um, guys, I hate to be a stickler for detail, but did we decide just how we're going to *stop* that tiger?" Samir asks.

"Not exactly," Hana says.

"That's what I thought," Samir sighs.

"Look for a drawing of a tiger," Ms. W says. "That's where Blake gets his power."

"You mean, like this one?" Heathcliff says, whipping out a folded piece of paper from his back pocket. It's one of Blake's drawings of a tiger. He must have swiped it from the church.

"You are a genius," I say, so relieved that I reach up and give him a kiss on the cheek. Temporarily taken aback, Heathcliff flushes slightly. I doubt there is anything cuter than a bad boy who blushes. "I told you he was on *our* side," I tell Ms. W and Coach H, who don't quite seem convinced yet.

"So that's why you found pieces of a tiger drawing

around campus," Hana says. "It must be Blake's way of turning himself back into a human again."

"But does he rip them up himself? And where does he carry them? In his tiger purse?" Samir asks.

"Technicalities," Hana says, waving her hand.

Another growl comes from the forest and I can tell the tiger is coming closer. I glance at the woods. I still can't see him, though.

"Not to be a downer, but we don't actually know if this works, do we?" Samir asks us, his eyes flitting back and forth between us and Ms. W and Coach H.

"No, but do you have any better ideas?" I ask him.

Suddenly I see a flash of orange and black in the woods to the left.

"He's there," I hiss, pointing.

"No, he's over there," Hana shouts, pointing in the other direction. We walk a little closer to the river. The glow from Ms. W casts a shadow on the water.

"Um, don't mind me, but I'm just going to go stand by the river. Cats don't like water, right?" Once he gets to the banks of the river, however, Samir stops short. "Um, guys," Samir says, in an unsure voice, "something's not right here."

That's when I notice that there's a red tint to the water.

"Blood," Hana hisses. "Blake has turned the river to blood. Just like in the Bible."

"He *what*?" Samir shouts, leaping away from the river's edge.

Before we can ponder this new development, a bright light appears above our heads. It's an angel. A real one. Unlike Blake's imaginary friend, this one we can see. He has great white wings and is wearing a white tunic and gold braided belt.

The angel doesn't speak, but it opens up an old scroll, and right before our eyes there's a bright ripple of light and the river starts to boil.

"That can't be good," I say.

Ms. W and Coach H seem to glow a bit brighter, shining their light on the bubbling river, and that's when I see a horse head rear up from the bloody water.

"Okay, I am so running away now," Samir says.

"Not so fast," Hana counters, grabbing Samir's arm.

As we watch, the horse becomes whole, and on its back there's a rider with a long cloak and a scythe that looks very much like Death. Death is followed by three more horses, each one looking like something straight out of a Tim Burton movie. One is just a skeleton holding bundles of what look like dried, shriveled cornstalks. One is all sickly and ill. And the last, most gruesome one is some kind of bloodied warrior, who is carrying the severed heads of some unfortunate souls.

"The four horsemen of the Apocalypse," Heathcliff says. "War, famine, pestilence, and death." We all look at him, shocked. "I *have* been to church," he adds. "Believe it or not."

Heathcliff is full of surprises. The boy barely speaks, and when he does, he elaborates on Bible verse.

"We can't let them come ashore," Coach H says. "They'll destroy the island, or more . . ."

"And just how are we supposed to stop them?" Samir asks.

But Ms. W and Coach H spring to action. They levitate in the air, spinning in and near the horsemen. They swoop down on them like giant birds, attacking them from all sides. It's only a temporary solution, though. They won't be able to hold them off forever.

"I don't suppose there's a magical Bible in the vault?" I ask Hana.

"Drawings," Hana says. "Blake has to have them somewhere. These are his creations."

"Arrrrggggggggh," shouts Samir, as the Pestilence horseman leans over and touches his sleeve. After just this one touch, Samir falls to the ground as if shot, his eyes closed and his breathing shallow. Red dots appear on his face. It's like instant plague.

"The boathouse!" I say, remembering that Blake kept drawings there. "We have to get Blake's drawings."

"You both go, I'll stay with Samir," Hana says, taking off her Bard blazer and folding it up as a pillow that she puts under his head.

Inside the boathouse seems deserted. It's dark, except for the light spilling in from the angel outside, sending odd shadows along the floor. It's like trying to find your way by the light of a fireworks show. Heathcliff looks around and seems to almost sniff the air, as if trying to track Blake by scent. Whatever he smells or doesn't smell, he seems to be satisfied. Together we climb the stairs, and at the top of the landing, Heathcliff turns to me and puts his finger to his lips to tell me to be quiet. Then he silently turns the knob of the office door. The door swings open with a slight creaking sound, and inside I'm surprised to see Blake's tiger sitting there, quietly, facing the door as if it were waiting for us. Its paw rests protectively on top of a stack of drawings.

"Blake," Heathcliff says. "Stop what you're doing. Now."

The tiger, however, just stares blankly at Heathcliff. It stretches its other paw out, lengthening its back and showing us its full dimensions. It's about the size of a couch.

"I warned you," Heathcliff says, whipping out the tiger drawing.

The tiger sits up and sniffs the air. Then it growls. Blake doesn't like the fact that Heathcliff has one of its drawings, that's for sure. Heathcliff begins to rip up the drawing, and that's when the tiger yelps, and then bright white cracks start to appear in its fur. The tiger is literally breaking apart.

"It's working," I cry, amazed.

Before it fades completely, the tiger kicks up the stack of drawings, sending some of them in our direction, but a few more, including some of the horsemen, fly out the open window and down to the dirt ground below. Drawings of tigers flitter to our feet. Before I can pick the pages up, another tiger leaps in through the window. It's followed by a second and a third. What the . . . ? There's more than one? So which one is Blake?

"Get out of here," Heathcliff hisses at me as he scoops to pick up some of the tiger drawings.

"But—"

"Go get the horsemen drawings," he tells me. "Save Samir." It's a command, not a request.

Reluctantly I leave Heathcliff, flying down the stairs and running outside. I see that Coach H and Ms. W are still trying to contain the horsemen, without much luck. In fact, there are only three of them. One is missing.

Hana and Samir are hiding behind a nearby boulder.

Samir is getting worse by the second. The pink spots on his face have turned into red welts, and even in the dim light I can tell he's in a great deal of pain.

I run over to the place where the drawings fell. I drop to my knees to pick them up, and as I grab three of them and reach for a fourth, the paper is suddenly pinned to the ground by a horse's hoof. That's when I glance up and see myself staring at the Death horseman, complete with black hood and scythe. I'm temporarily paralyzed, and all I can do is watch, helplessly, as he leans over and touches my shoulder with one bony finger.

Twenty-nine

I squeeze my eyes shut and prepare for the worst. This is it—the end. I saw what happened to Samir. One touch from Pestilence and he came down with the plague. I'm sure Death is even more efficient.

Am I going to see my life flash before my eyes? Or will I see a big bright light? Or—heaven forbid—am I going to find myself stuck at Bard—as a ghost student—for all eternity? I'm really hoping that God has other plans for me. If I have to be stuck in purgatory, please make it on some tropical island somewhere. Maybe something like *Lost,* only without the "others" and with more cute young guys. Like Ryan. Or Heathcliff.

And that's when I realize that a good ten seconds have gone by and I'm not dead. I open my eyes and glance up. Yes, Death is standing above me. Yes, he touched me. But I'm unaffected. I *didn't* die. I don't even feel sick.

"Nice try," I tell Death, who smells, well, a lot like roadkill. Quickly I snatch up his drawing and rip it to pieces. His face and arms are suddenly beginning to crack, each wrinkle filled with bright light brimming up from beneath, as if he's going to explode. Instead he just falls to torn pieces that glow briefly on the ground before they turn to ash. I dispatch the other horsemen just as easily, and Ms. W and Coach H seem surprised for a moment, and then see the pieces of the drawings in my hand and give me nods of approval. After Pestilence is destroyed, Samir comes to with a groggy moan.

"God, what happened? I have the worst hangover ever." He groans, holding his head as if he's afraid it might fall apart.

"You almost died, you big idiot," Hana cries, and then throws her arms around Samir in a hug so tight that Samir can't breathe. When she realizes what she's doing, she drops her arms, and instead winds up and gives Samir a hard punch in the shoulder.

"Ow! What was that for? I nearly *died*." Samir groans again.

"Exactly! You almost died and left me, you jerk," Hana says.

"Why didn't Death kill me?" I ask Ms. W, who approaches and puts her arm around me.

She studies me for a second. "You're different from Samir," she says. "You have roots in both this world and the fictional one. So he didn't have the same power over you."

Wow. Finally a perk of having a great-great-great grandmother who's a fictional character.

"Where's Blake?" Coach H asks me, shaking off droplets of water from the river, which has turned back, thankfully, to a normal water color.

Just then, we hear a crashing sound coming from the boathouse. I'd completely forgotten about Heathcliff.

I'm the first to scramble up the stairs, although Coach H and Ms. W don't bother with them (they simply float straight up through the floor of the boathouse office). Inside I see Heathcliff cornered by Blake—not Blake the tiger, but Blake as his normal self. Blake has opened the locket and has the tiny remaining corner of *Wuthering Heights* out, and is holding it precariously between two fingers. Heathcliff is temporarily frozen, not sure whether to leap on him or stay put.

"Stay back! All of you," shouts Blake. He seems to have a kind of wild look in his eye.

"Blake, you have to stop what you're doing," Ms. W says in her most calm voice. "No good will come of it."

Coach H tries to work his way to the other side of Blake, but Blake whirls. "I said *back*," he shouts, waving the piece of paper in front of him. I'm surprised Ms. W and Coach H don't just sweep forward. It's not like they would mind if Heathcliff is sent back to *Wuthering Heights.*

"This is not part of God's plan," Blake mumbles to himself. "This place is an abomination."

"What place? Bard?" I ask him. If I can keep him talking then he won't destroy the paper.

"Obviously," he says. "I was a faithful servant of God. I do not deserve to be stuck in limbo. I ought to be in heaven with my darling wife. Heaven was promised to me by Gabriele! Limbo is for sinners. Dante's sinners. And the very nature of this place is a sacrilege. That church is an insult to God. I spent my life working in the glory of the Lord. All my poetry and artistry dedicated to His great power."

Okay, he's clearly gone off the deep end.

"But you yourself know that God's will can't be known," Ms. W says. "Your tiger represents the unknowable and often contradictory nature of God. He didn't just create the peaceful lamb. He also created the fierce killer, the tiger. It proves you can't really understand God's motives."

"Yes, but . . ."

"And if God is truly mysterious, then He could have created a place like this. To test people like you, and people like us."

Blake is temporarily calmed by this new thought. He lowers his arms, as if trying to process this new information.

"But . . . Gabriele told me," he says, looking up to a space above our heads.

"Did you actually *see* Gabriele?" Coach H asks.

"No, but I heard her," Blake says. "She spoke to me."

"She? I thought Gabriele was a man," Hana says.

"Emily," Ms. W hisses under her breath to Coach H. Does she mean Emily Brontë? The ghost who just last semester tried to free all her fictional characters, nearly destroying our dimension as we know it. Could she have survived the destruction of her book? Then again, Heathcliff is here because part of one page survived. Maybe Emily is, too, only she's invisible to most of us. Or chooses to be.

"Did you know about this? Is Emily still with us?" Coach H thunders at Heathcliff, but Heathcliff looks just as surprised as the rest of us.

"She's the stalker," I cry, struck by a sudden thought. "What if it was Emily Brontë wearing the sweatshirt and running around campus causing mischief? Heathcliff was tied up, but Emily—as a ghost— could have taken nearly any form she wanted. That would explain why the Hooded Sweatshirt Stalker didn't have a face. Maybe Emily had enough power in this plane to fill out clothes, but not much else."

"Emily?" Blake echoes. "Emily Brontë?"

"We think you've been misled," Ms. W says softly. "We think the angel you thought was Gabriele might have been the voice of Emily Brontë. She's wanted to destroy this campus and she used you as her pawn. She's the one who told you what you wanted to hear."

Blake slumps forward, the piece of *Wuthering Heights* and my locket slipping from his grasp. Coach H sweeps forward, picking up both items. Ms. W puts her arm around Blake, who seems to be crying.

"I think the danger's over," Ms. W tells us.

"But what about Emily?" I ask. "She's still on the loose."

"She clearly needs help to do any damage, or she wouldn't have involved Blake," Ms. W says. "There's nothing we can do now but tell Headmaster B about what's transpired."

"That means show's over, folks," Coach H tells us.

Thirty

"I *missed* the horsemen of the Apocalypse?" cries Blade when I find her in our room the next day and fill her in on the near ending of the world she just missed. "Oh my God, I am going to *die*."

As I suspected, my Goth roomie is very sorry to have missed Death and Pestilence.

"Where were you anyway?" Hana asks her, standing in our doorway and eyeing Blade's Satan poster.

"Duh—with Number Thirty-one," she says. "We were having sex in his room."

"Um, and just how did you get away from the Guardians? How did you avoid the room sweeps?" I couldn't get two minutes alone with Ryan, and here is my roomie doing the dirty with Number Thirty-one.

"I have my ways," Blade says. "Like an invisibility spell."

"Does your 'invisibility spell' have anything to do with hiding in Number Thirty-one's closet?"

"It might," Blade says.

"So you didn't see the tiger?" Hana asks, disbelieving.

"Nope," Blade says, shaking her head.

"God, you missed *everything*," Hana says. "So much for your psychic Wiccan witch powers." Hana nods toward Blade's witch graduation diploma on her wall.

"I'm not psychic," Blade says. "If I had ESP, then I would've known Number Thirty-one is a waste of time because he has a pecker the size of a . . ." Blade holds up her pinkie finger.

"Ew," Hana and I both say at once.

"That's TMI," I add.

"God—I can't *believe* I missed the horse dudes," Blade exclaims, punching her pillow. "Were they cool? Tell me everything."

"They weren't cool. Pestilence nearly killed Samir," Hana says.

"Pestilence! Ugh—and I missed it!" Blade says, flopping down on her bed and covering her face with her pillow.

"So how do you think they're going to explain the tiger?" Hana asks me, ignoring Blade's theatrics.

"They don't have to," Blade says, holding up the

latest edition of the *Bard Weekly*. "There's already a rumor that it escaped from a ship carrying a zoo across the Atlantic."

The newspaper's headlines read "Tiger Escapes from Zoo Ship" and "Headmaster B Subdues Tiger with Folding Chair."

"Did she really kick the tiger's butt with a *chair*?" Blade asks.

"Pretty much," Hana says.

"Don't you think parents will be upset?" I ask.

"Uh, did you forget where we are?" Hana asks me. "The parents who sent their kids here don't care." Hana looks down at her hands. She speaks from personal experience, considering her parentals seem to always take neglect to the next level.

"Do you know what's going to happen to Heathcliff?" Hana asks me.

"I don't know," I say. This much is true. Ms. W and Coach H took him with them to see Headmaster B. Ms. W promised they wouldn't hurt him, and that I'd be summoned later. I remember the look on Heathcliff's face, though. He seemed resigned to whatever they decided. I can't help but worry. I'm not even fully enjoying my new freedom. Ms. W took away my red vest and told me I'm once again allowed to mix with the Bard masses.

"By the way, speaking of beefcakes, you'll be happy

to know that Ryan's going to be okay," Blade says. "He had a mild concussion and he'll be hanging out in the infirmary for a couple of days, but should be fine."

I'd been so worried about Heathcliff, I temporarily forgot about Ryan. What does that say about me? What kind of girlfriend—I mean, ex-girlfriend—am I?

Down at the bottom of the front page of the newspaper, there's a small story saying they've caught the Hooded Sweatshirt Stalker. Hana taps that story with her finger.

"What is Parker going to do without a stalker around?" she asks. "She doesn't have an excuse to stalk Ryan."

"I'm guessing she's not happy," I reply.

"That karma, she's a bitch," Blade adds. "So are you going to give up the details about the horsemen? Or am I going to have to beg?"

"Begging would be nice," I say.

"Don't make me put a hex on you," Blade says.

That afternoon, Ms. W takes me to Headmaster B's office.

"Ms. W, I was wondering," I say.

"Yes?"

"Before you disappeared, you tried to tell me something about my future here at Bard. What did you mean?"

Ms. W gives me a sidelong glance.

"I think you'll find things out in your own time."

"But is there something you know—that the faculty knows—and aren't telling me?" I think back to the bombshell that I'm part fiction. The faculty knew and didn't say. What else do they know about me?

Ms. W sighs.

"There's some speculation that you're going to be a writer. A very good writer," Ms. W says.

"Me?" I ask. "But Coach H just accused me of plagiarizing."

"He knows you didn't do that. But Parker put him in a difficult position," Ms. W says. "But, more importantly, you'd be the first prominent writer with fictional roots. No one knows what this could mean. But it would be a first."

"How do you know I'll be a good writer?"

"Let's just say that writers know their own," Ms. W says. "We can smell them a mile away. And if you'd like, I'd like to tutor you. Mentor you, even."

"So if I become a famous writer, then you get some good karma points and get one step closer to getting out of this place?"

"You see right through me," Ms. W says, smiling. "That's the first step in being a good writer. Being a good observer."

"So the lessons are already starting then?" I say.

"Does this mean you're going to be my Mr. Miyagi? Wax on. Wax off?"

"Mr. Who?" Ms. W asks. Sometimes I forget that her pop culture references only extend to 1941.

"So are you going to tell me what Headmaster B decided to do with Heathcliff? Or do I have to guess?"

"You'll find out shortly," Ms. W says. "It's a fair decision."

In Headmaster B's office, I see a subdued Heathcliff sitting quietly in a chair, staring at Headmaster B, who is sitting behind her desk with her arms crossed. Heathcliff's dark, curly hair is back from his face and he looks like he's shaved. The Bard uniform barely fits his broad shoulders.

"Miranda—sit," Headmaster B says. I take the open seat next to Heathcliff. I look over at his face, trying to read it, but as usual it's a blank slate. Correction: a frowning slate. He doesn't like authority figures, least of all Headmaster B—the sister of his creator, Emily Brontë.

"First of all, I owe you an apology," Headmaster B says. "We unfairly accused and convicted you of meddling in the disappearance of two of our faculty members. For that, I apologize."

"Apology accepted," I say.

"Now, before us is the more serious issue of you

withholding information about Heathcliff," Headmaster B says. "And, more generally, about Heathcliff's future."

I glance over at Heathcliff, but he's just staring at his shoes. "I think it's important for you to know how helpful he was these past few weeks," I blurt. "Not only would I have been dead, but most of the students, if it wasn't for Heathcliff—"

Headmaster B waves her arm to show she doesn't want to hear more. "I know, Ms. Tate," she says, unable to keep a little annoyance from her voice. "But what's more important, Miranda, is that you no longer keep secrets like this from us in the future. It's important that we be able to trust you."

"I understand," I say. "I promise."

"Good," she says and nods her head. "Now, the faculty have met to discuss the fate of Heathcliff. And we've decided that, for now . . . he can stay."

"He can stay!" I shout, elated. Without meaning to, I lean over and hug Heathcliff. He's temporarily taken aback, but then he folds his arms around me.

"Ahem," Headmaster B says, clearing her throat. "Contain yourself, Ms. Tate," she commands before continuing. "There are three conditions under which he can stay. He cannot leave the school grounds, which basically encompass this island. His stay here can only be three years, as that's the length of time he is missing from the novel *Wuthering Heights*. And he's already spent eight months of that time here."

"That's all!" I cry. That's hardly fair. He can only stay in this world, well, until I graduate.

"Also, Ms. Tate, it is *very* important that he not form any *romantic* entanglements while here."

She stares at me pointedly.

"But—"

"If we see or hear of *anything,* ahem, *untoward* going on between you two, we will have no choice but to banish Heathcliff immediately," she says. "This is for Heathcliff's own good. When it is time for him to return to the novel, he *has* to go. Are we agreed, Mr. Heathcliff?"

Heathcliff looks at his shoes and nods. I think about the kiss he landed on me in the secret passageway. I feel a pang of disappointment.

"Are we agreed, Ms. Tate?" Headmaster B asks me.

I look at Heathcliff and then at Headmaster B. I see no alternative. Reluctantly, I nod.

Outside Headmaster B's office, Heathcliff turns and looks at me.

"Thank you," he says.

"For what?" I don't think I did anything other than agree to let them send him back to *Wuthering Heights* in two years and four months. It hardly seems like a good ending.

"For believing in me," he says.

"But they'll only let you stay two years and four months," I say. "That's so unfair. And we . . . I mean, we can't . . ." What? Kiss? Date? Get it on like rabbits? No words seem appropriate here, so I just trail off awkwardly.

Heathcliff gently takes my hand and turns it over in his palm, as if studying it. Then, ever so gently, he bends down and kisses the upside of my wrist.

"Any time I can spend with you, I'm grateful for," he says. He gives me a piercing look.

The spell is broken by the approach of Coach H. "So I hear I need to find a room for you," Coach H tells Heathcliff, clapping him on the shoulder and pulling him away from me. "Let's get started with that, shall we?"

I watch the two of them walk across campus. Every so often, Heathcliff turns back to look at me.

I can feel the spot on my wrist he kissed. It tingles.

So much for no romantic entanglements, I think.

Thirty-one

"Your love life is more convoluted than *The OC*," Hana tells me as we walk together across campus.

"Tell me about it. What am I supposed to do?" I've confessed to Hana that I think I have feelings for both Ryan and Heathcliff.

"Well, considering that romance with Heathcliff is forbidden, and he's from 1847, you know my pick would be Ryan."

"Who knows if he would even take me back?" I ask, still not sure how I feel about Ryan. Do I even want to be his girlfriend again? I just don't know. How sad is that?

"You don't know until you try," Hana says.

"I don't know what to do," I say, thinking about the place on my wrist where Heathcliff kissed.

"You'd better figure it out quickly," Hana says.

"We're here." Hana stops outside the infirmary, where I've come to visit Ryan. After his run-in with a tiger, he's been resting until Coach H is sure he's ready to go back to class.

"I don't know what to say," I say.

"Start with 'how are you feeling?' and go from there," Hana says.

"You mean if he doesn't throw me out first," I say.

"Just *go*," Hana huffs, giving me a little shove inside.

Ryan is sitting up in a cot. He's got his head bandaged, but otherwise, he looks good. He's talking to Derek Mann when I get there.

"Miranda!" Ryan says, his face lighting up when he sees me. I'm surprised. I wasn't sure what I was expecting, but this definitely isn't it.

"Hi, Ryan. Um, how are you feeling?" I ask, taking Hana's advice.

"Good," he says. "I'm glad you came."

"You are?" I ask, still surprised. Just last week he hated me.

"Of course I am. You saved my *life*," he says. "If you hadn't distracted that tiger when I was helping Parker, we'd have both been goners."

I guess that part is true. "But you saved my life right back," I say. "So we're even."

"I don't know about even," Ryan says. "I can't believe how brave you were. You weren't afraid of that tiger at all. Unlike Derek here."

Derek turns bright red. "I wasn't afraid."

"No, you were petrified," Ryan corrects. "Speaking of Derek, I think he has something to say to you."

Derek Mann clears his throat and looks at his shoes. Ryan gives him a nudge.

"Uh, yeah. Um, I, uh . . . I'm sorry," Derek Mann says.

Are my ears working? Did Derek "the" Mann just *apologize*? That's a first. And I thought since his public abstinence pledge, I'd seen it all.

"You're sorry for . . .?" Ryan prompts.

"For, uh . . . believing those rumors about you. And, uh, helping to spread them. I know now they're not true. Mr. B suggested I write the column, and well . . ."

So Blake was behind that, too!

"And I'm going to write an op-ed piece for the student newspaper, explaining how the rumor was all wrong, and how we were wrong to ostracize you over something so stupid."

"Well," I say, glancing over at Ryan. I know this is all his doing. "Thank you, Derek. Apology accepted."

Derek mumbles something I can't quite hear and then leaves the room. Clearly Derek "the" Mann isn't used to apologizing to anyone.

"How did you get him to do that?" I ask Ryan.

"I threatened to write a letter exposing the fact that he's a virgin."

"He's a *virgin*?" I cry, and I can't help it—I laugh. "But the rumors. The reputation that he's a ladies' man?"

"All lies. His doing. I don't think he even kissed a girl for the first time until two months ago."

"But what about him supposedly knocking up the principal's daughter—at his old school?"

"Total fabrication," Ryan says. "I don't know what the real reason is, but I think it had to do with the fact that he threw a party at his house when his parents weren't home. Only I don't think anybody *came*. I heard that he ordered a big keg, but it just sat there, sweating on his parents' living room rug."

I have to laugh at that. A free keg—and still nobody showed up? How unpopular do you have to be for that to happen?

"Wow," I say. "I guess you really can't believe rumors."

"Exactly my point all along," Ryan says.

I can see with perfect clarity that I've treated Ryan terribly. He really is a good guy.

"Listen, Ryan, I'm really sorry for everything that's happened. I think you were right. I overreacted."

Ryan smiles and then looks down at his hands, folded in his lap.

"Look, it's no problem, really," Ryan says. "It helped me do some thinking actually. I was thinking that maybe we should start over," he says. My heart skips a beat. He *does* still want to be my boyfriend. A tiny voice in my head says, What about Heathcliff?

I am such a headcase. A boy-crazy headcase. Still, if Ryan is willing to give us another shot, then shouldn't I be open to that possibility, too?

"Yes, I think so, too," I say.

"Hear me out," Ryan says. He glances down at his hands. "Miranda, I *really* like you."

"I *really* like you, too," I say.

"But . . ."

"But?" I echo. Where did the "but" come from? "Buts" are never good.

"But, I think maybe we ought to just be friends."

The words hit my stomach like a bowling ball. Just friends?

"I mean, I've had more experience than you. And I'm older, and maybe, well, I just don't think we're a good fit right now. Maybe things will change, but I think we want different things right now. And I think I rushed things with you."

"You mean sex?" I cry. "It'll be different this time, I'm—" I was about to say "ready," but Ryan cuts me off.

"No," Ryan says, shaking his head. "Be honest with me. You don't even know what you want."

This is true. But I'm fifteen (sixteen in less than twenty-four hours). Am I supposed to know everything right now?

Ryan pulls me forward, and just when I think he might kiss me on the lips and make everything he's said go away, he gives me a peck on the forehead. Like I was his kid sister. It feels like a slap.

"Let's just be friends for now, and see how things go?" he suggests.

"Ouch," Hana says, when I fill her in on the details as she and I and Samir walk to the mailroom to pick up our mail.

"The friend speech—I *hate* that speech," Samir seconds.

"I just don't get it," I say, shaking my head. "I mean, I go from having two boyfriends to none. How is that fair?"

"It isn't," Hana agrees.

"I mean, I save the world, but I don't get the boy? How is that *fair*?"

"Whoa—*you* saved the world! What about us?" Hana cries.

"Okay, *we* saved the world," I amend, putting my arm around Hana.

"Yeah, don't forget me, either," Samir says.

"Oh yeah, a lot of good you did nearly dying," Hana says.

"Hey! I'd like to see how well you deal with the plague," he shoots back. "Besides, it's called being a *martyr*. Look it up."

"Guys! We *all* saved the world, okay? I stand corrected."

In my mailbox, I find one letter and two brightly colored envelopes. The two envelopes are from Mom and Lindsay—they're birthday cards.

At least they remembered. In her card, Mom promises to throw me a party in June, when I'm back home. It won't be like the *My Super Sweet 16* bashes on MTV, but frankly, a trip to Pizza Hut would seem like a luxury after another few months of Bard food.

Lindsay's card is about sisters who borrow each other's shoes. It would be funny except that I know Lindsay is totally raiding my closet right now, and she has Fred Flintstone feet.

The last envelope is from my dad. Did he actually send me a birthday card? I open the envelope to discover a folded letter.

Miranda,

Your stepmother Carmen has suggested that a summer job might prove you're mature enough to drive, and she has been generous enough to offer you work at her new clothing boutique. To make up what you spent on her credit card, you won't be getting a salary, but will be working a minimum of 35 hours a week. Any complaints or back talk from you on this issue and I will report your theft of my car to the police.

I've talked this over with your mother, and she's reluctantly agreed that working might be the best thing for you.

Sincerely,
Dad

Happy birthday to me.

I doubt he even remembered.

I can't believe I'm going to be Carmen's slave for the entire summer. I'd rather deal with the horsemen of the Apocalypse, thanks. And since when did she have the money to open up her own clothing store? Now I *know* that had to come from my college fund.

Slowly I ball up the letter in my hands until it's the size of a big gumball.

"Bad news?" Hana asks me.

"Just my dad—ruining my life as usual," I say through gritted teeth.

"How do parents always know *just* how to do that?" Samir asks, holding up a letter from his mother. It's got a picture of his would-be wife, the girl his mom has arranged for him to marry when he turns nineteen.

"At least your parents bother to write," Hana says, tilting her head toward her empty mailbox.

"I'd *prefer* the silent treatment, are you kidding?" Samir says, echoing my own thoughts.

I have to agree. It was better when Dad just ignored me.

Thirty-two

The morning of my sixteenth birthday, I wake up feeling like my life is already over. How am I ever going to survive an entire summer as Carmen's slave? I can't even tolerate her company for fifteen minutes without wanting to slash my wrists. Not to mention, she is only twenty-four. What could she possibly have to teach me?

"Happy birthday!" Blade chirps at me. I blink away eye sleepies and see that Blade has decorated our room while I slept. I don't know what is more sweet—the fact that she remembered my birthday, or that she sacrificed her regular eleven hours of sleep to do it.

"I have a special birthday gift for you," she says, pulling a small satchel from behind her back. "It's a spell. You wear it around your neck."

I sniff it warily. Usually Blade's "spells" smell like feet. This one, however, smells like apples.

"What's it supposed to do?" I say as I put the small beaded rope around my neck.

"It's supposed to make your true love come back to you," she says.

"But Ryan says he just wants to be friends."

"Not after he gets a whiff of *this,* he won't," Blade says, sounding certain. I have absolutely no confidence that it will work, but it's thoughtful all the same.

"Thanks, Blade," I say, and I give her a hug.

"Ew! What was that for?" she asks me, squirming away from the hug.

"Sorry," I say, but I notice even Blade, who is opposed to anything approaching a mushy emotional moment, can't help but smile a little.

At breakfast, Hana and Samir have somehow gotten a Hostess Ding Dong cake from somewhere, and they've put a match in it for a candle. They light the match outside the cafeteria and put it in the chocolate Ding Dong, and sing "Happy Birthday to You" as I blow it out.

Outside it's a warm and sunny day, which is the best kind of birthday, and after I chow down on the Ding Dong, Hana, Samir, and Blade wander off to their classes, while I'm left in the commons. My class (theology) doesn't meet today because Coach H has given us all "research paper" assignments, so we're supposed to do research in the library.

I, however, feel much more like sunning myself on the commons, which is what I do, as I lay out my Bard blazer on the green grass and plop down with the hundreds of history pages I have to read (I am so far behind it's not even funny). I read a little bit about Queen Elizabeth and then my attention starts to wander, and I find myself looking around me. There are a few other students on the grass, even as Guardians take up impromptu posts by some trees to watch us. You can't go anywhere at Bard without someone watching.

I glance over toward the infirmary, and that's when I see Ryan Kent coming out. He's alone, and he blinks back a little against the sun, and then, for a second, I think he sees me. I give him a tentative wave (we're supposed to be friends, aren't we?) and then he waves back, and seems to be coming in my direction.

I finger the spell satchel Blade gave me. Could it actually be working?

I glance around to see if maybe he might be walking toward Parker or someone else, and that's when I see Heathcliff, coming up from the other end of the commons, and walking right toward me.

Okay, Blade didn't say anything about attracting *two* true loves. I glance back at Ryan. He's about the same distance as Heathcliff and they're walking at the same pace. I'm no whiz at physics, but it looks like they're going to reach me at about the same time.

I have a sudden flash of a word problem: Your ex-boyfriend is heading toward you at a speed of five miles per hour from the north. Your forbidden boyfriend (of sorts) is heading toward you from the south at five miles per hour. Which one will get to you first, and on a scale of one to ten, just how awkward is this encounter going to be?

I watch in slow motion as the two boys halve and then quarter the distance between them and me.

It's Heathcliff that reaches me first.

He doesn't say anything, being a boy of few words. He just plops down next to me, pushing his dark hair out of his eyes. Ryan, four feet from me, stops, eyes Heathcliff, and then suddenly changes direction, heading off toward the library. He doesn't even miss a beat. He simply pretends he had never planned to stop. I can't help but feel a pang of disappointment.

Next to me, Heathcliff reaches into his pocket. He pulls out the locket that contains the piece of *Wuthering Heights.*

"How did you get this?" I cry, grabbing it from his hand.

He only shrugs. I can't help but notice that he's watching the retreating figure of Ryan Kent, heading away from us. Heathcliff pulls his attention from Ryan and then back to me.

"Happy birthday," he tells me, taking the locket back as he fastens the chain around my neck. His fingers just brush the base of my neck as he does so, and they feel warm.

"But how did you know it was my birthday?"

Heathcliff stares at me without blinking. "Don't you know by now? I know everything about you," he says.

I glance up at him, and he's just inches from me, so close to me that I can see his eyelashes. They're long and dark and thick. There's another surprise, I think. Heathcliff has girl lashes. Who knew?

Our noses are nearly touching and all I can think is what his lips will taste like, when abruptly, he pulls away from me. He's looking over my shoulder, and I turn and see that Coach H has spied us and is giving us a disapproving look.

When I turn back around toward Heathcliff, he's already picked himself up off the grass and is walking away from me.

"But . . ." I start, even though I know it's already too late. Heathcliff is off, just as quickly as he came.

I run my fingers over the smooth gold locket hanging outside my Bard shirt, and watch Heathcliff until he turns the corner around Macduff dorm, and I can't see him anymore.

From two boys to none—in five seconds flat.

That has got to be a new record.

Your attitude. Your style.
MTV Books:
Totally your type.

Cruel Summer
First in the Fast Girls, Hot Boys series!

Kylie Adams

Life is a popularity contest...and someone is about to lose. In sexy Miami Beach, five friends are wrapping up high school—but one of them won't make it to graduation alive....

The Pursuit of Happiness
Tara Altebrando

Declare your independence....After her mother dies and her boyfriend cheats on her, Betsy picks up the pieces of her devastated life and finds remarkable strength and unexpected passion.

Life as a Poser
First in the *310* series!

Beth Killian

Sometimes you have to fake it to make it....Eva spends an intoxicating summer in glamorous Hollywood with her famous talent agent aunt in this witty, pop culture-savvy novel, first in a new series.

Plan B
Jenny O'Connell

Plan A didn't know about him....When her movie-star half brother—a total teen heartthrob—comes to town, one very practical girl's plans for graduation and beyond are blown out of the water.

Available wherever books are sold.

MTV BOOKS

Published by Pocket Books
A Division of Simon & Schuster
A CBS Company

www.simonsays.com/mtvbooks

14330